Murder on Biltmore Way

Murder on Biltmore Way

A case of Detective María Duquesne

by Uva de Aragón

Translated by
Jeffrey C. Barnett and Kathleen Bulger-Barnett

Published by Eriginal Books LLC

Miami, Florida

ISBN 978-1-61370-123-2

Previous Editions:

El crimen de Biltmore Way, Miami; Eriginal Book, 2020

Support for the publication of this work was provided by the Class of 1956 Provost's Faculty Development Endowment at Washington and Lee University.

For Jeff and Kathleen Barnett,
friends, translators, and accomplices,
for everything and then some

Chapter 1: The Scene

Day 1, Monday

As she usually did, María Duquesne glanced at herself in the mirror before leaving her house and she smiled at her reflection. Four years earlier, she had decided to lose some weight and she'd been able to do so thanks to her spinning classes. At first, she found it difficult to make it through the entire hour despite the fact that the music and the instructor could not have been better. Nevertheless, once her body started getting used to it, she felt bad if she missed class two days in a row. She also had to give up snacking, but working out regularly helped maintain her new figure.

The detective was restless. Three years had passed since she had closed the case involving the death of Alberto González and the baby who had disappeared in 1992. Since then, all the cases assigned to her had been solved quickly. That's not to say that some of them weren't awful, like the man found under the elevated train tracks stabbed to death with a three-foot long machete. In fewer than forty-eight hours, they had arrested the suspect, a resident from the same homeless shelter where the victim was staying. She had also been busy with heartbreaking cases, like the one of a grandmother who had been run over. It took them less than a day to catch the driver, who had tried to get away.

According to the statistics, crime had gone down, but it didn't seem that way to María. The majority of murders were being committed by men against their own family members. There had even been people killed over a parking space. Miami was no longer the peaceful city where she had grown up. The constant traffic, among other things, had everybody on edge.

Worst of all were the mass public shootings. It was something that had finally hit close to home in Parkland high school. The perpetrators almost always committed suicide, but that wasn't the case with this particular young man who had killed more than seventeen people, among them students and teachers, and he had also injured an equal number. In every single case, the politicians expressed their sympathy, and they said to pray for the victims and their families, but they didn't do anything despite the pressure from the community. Some blamed the problem on mental illness, others on a lack of gun control. María tried to do her work and not argue or think much about things that were out of her control.

None of her recent cases had taken months or even weeks to solve. *They hadn't been full of intrigue either*, she thought as she drove to the station that Monday morning. As if someone had heard her thoughts, just then she received a call from headquarters. They had found a woman's body in an apartment on Biltmore Way in Coral Gables.

"I'm on my way right now."

As soon as they gave her the address, she knew it was the same building that used to be an old hotel and some years ago was converted into condominiums. More than twenty years ago, she had gone there with her parents and grandmother, both to the rooftop Club and the French restaurant on the main floor, one of her mother's favorites.

It surprised her that the lobby hadn't changed much. It still had that somewhat over-the-top style that she thought was elegant back in the day. Now it just seemed somewhat gaudy. But actually, that was the least of her concerns right now. She was anxious to get underway with the investigation.

The lobby was swarming with police and residents, all talking about how unusual it was for something like this to happen in Coral Gables, and even more so in a building with a doorman and security cameras.

As she entered the crime scene, María was surprised that nothing seemed to be out of place. The apartment was decorated in good taste with high quality, contemporary furniture and an abundance of artwork on the walls. It was one of the best units in the entire building, with two bedrooms, two baths, and a balcony that overlooked the golf course. The woman's body was in the master bedroom. She immediately noticed that she had been delicately placed on the bed after she was killed, which led her to believe that the murderer was somebody that knew her. She was dressed. She was almost certain that she had not been raped or sexually assaulted.

Her assistant, Ivan Fernández, had arrived a few minutes earlier and brought her up to speed.

"Her name is Sarah Turner. Thirty-five years old. She is—well, *was*—a decorator, art collector, and vendor. She bought this condo three years ago. Before that she lived in New York."

"She's incredibly beautiful," María added as she came closer to the body while the photographers took pictures of the dead woman and the forensic team gathered pertinent evidence.

"There aren't any signs of violence, right?" the detective asked.

"None that we have found, so far," Fernández answered, "but I certainly don't think that she died from natural causes," he added ironically. "Besides, when they found her, she was already covered up with this blanket."

"Which leads me to believe that it was somebody that knew her."

"I can't confirm anything until we get the autopsy back, but there's every indication that she died from a severe blow to the head."

The forensic doctor cradled the dead woman's head in his gloved hands, and he showed them the blood that oozed from the gash in her skull and matted her long blonde hair.

"What do you think the time of death was?"

"It's been at least twelve hours, maybe some time between 5:00 p.m. and 7:00 p.m. yesterday, Sunday, but like I said before, I'll be able to be more precise after the autopsy."

The detective felt that flutter in her chest that a new difficult case always brought about. She had witnessed many crime scenes that were truly grotesque. Here, on the other hand, everything in the apartment was in order and the young dead woman merely appeared to be asleep. María felt a slight chill, as if the disconnect between the crime scene and the murder had produced some type of confusing angst.

She swallowed her feelings and got to work. She interviewed Aura, the Nicaraguan woman who had found the body. She usually came by once a week to clean and do the laundry. Sometimes Miss Turner took off early or was away on a trip, and if no one answered the door, she had a key to the apartment and would let herself in. She couldn't imagine who would have wanted to hurt such a nice lady. Aura seemed nervous, but with all of María's experience reading people, she knew right away that the woman was acting uneasy because she had found the body, not because she was involved or had anything to hide. In any case, she asked her to stay a bit longer. Perhaps she could be of some help. As it turned out, Aura told them that Miss Turner's parents lived in New York... that she occasionally visited them... and they sometimes came to Miami... that she had a sister... that Miss Turner worked for several companies decorating apartments or model homes, the foyers of commercial buildings, offices... No, she didn't have a boyfriend, at least as far as she knew... such a beautiful and intelligent young woman. Well, she did have one, but she hadn't seen her with anybody in a long time. Miss Turner was very organized... so all she had to do was clean and wash the clothes. Everything was always in its place. Yes, she had a cell that she was always either talking or texting on... and also a small computer... or maybe two. No, she didn't have many visitors, although sometimes she had people over for dinner.

Ivan informed her that everything in the apartment was in order, but he had placed two wine glasses in the evidence envelope.

"They were in the sink. Maybe we can extract some DNA and find out if she had somebody over," he explained.

"Thanks. I think we should notify the family," María said out loud, even though it was really meant for herself. It was one aspect of her job that she still found difficult. She decided to call the sister first. The woman told her that she was driving, and María paused.

"Do you think there's a way you could park the car and talk for a moment so you're not distracted?"

"Hold on a second. Let me see."

When María told her the news, the sister went silent. It took her a few seconds to react. As she sobbed, her voice cracked:

"It can't be... it just can't be. Are you sure it's her?"

"We need someone to come down and formally identify the body, but I can send a photo to your cell."

"Have you spoken with my parents?"

"No, I thought it'd be better to call you first."

"But how can I possibly tell them?"

"If you prefer, I can notify them... It's just that they should find out soon. We haven't released her name yet to the press, but they could still find out and publish it, or speak about the case, or reveal the address. Your parents shouldn't find out like that."

"Okay, can you send me the photo right now? I'm going to put you on speaker while I look at it... Oh my God, it's her... But she looks like she's asleep. Are you sure that she's dead?"

"Yes, I'm so sorry. It's important for the family to come as soon as possible. I assure you that we will do everything within our power to find the guilty party, but we need to ask the three of you some questions first. Are your parents in good health?"

"Yes, fortunately. They're not really that old. My mother just turned sixty-two and my father is two years older. But this is going to be such a terrible shock..."

Colleen Turner agreed to call María as soon as she had spoken with her parents and they had bought their tickets for Miami. The detective promised that she would get in touch with her if there were any updates that she should know about, although she stressed that the investigation was barely underway.

María and Fernández spent an hour interviewing the neighbors, but no one had seen anything suspicious. On a Monday morning, many people weren't home, so they decided to return after 6:00 p.m. By then, the doorman who had been on duty that Sunday would be back at work. Likewise, the manager agreed to let them take the security tapes from that weekend so they could examine them more thoroughly.

Back at the station, Fernández inspected Sarah Turner's iPad and laptop while María went over her cell phone. They listened to a message from the night before left by someone named Betty who asked her if she wanted to go out to get a bite to eat. She finished by saying: "well, if you have better company than me, then good for you…"

Betty turned out to be Sarah's neighbor and friend. She had already heard what had happened, and when María called her she could tell that she'd been crying. They agreed that María and Fernández would come by her house that evening to interview her. Less than an hour later, Colleen called to let them know that she and her parents were leaving at 6:00 in the evening and they would be in Miami by 9:00 that night. They were going to stay at the Biltmore Hotel. María asked her to let her know once they were settled at the hotel and for them to decide whether they wanted her to come see them then, or if they preferred to rest and begin everything in the morning. Her sister went ahead and authorized María to give Sarah's name to the press.

"If it helps, please do so."

María and Fernández had just come back from grabbing a sandwich and espresso at the café on the corner next to the station when they heard that Mr. Eric Anderson was waiting for them. Considered a mogul in the real estate world, he appeared quite often in the press, either inaugurating a new project or attending some glitzy gala for charity.

The boss, Larry Kepler, wasn't in yet, and the receptionist made the unusual decision to have Mr. Anderson wait in his office. She probably did so because a man of his stature—elegant, well mannered, and with an upper-class way of dressing and expressing himself—didn't typically frequent police headquarters.

When she and her colleague walked in, Mr. Anderson stood up and extended his hand, but María made a gesture for him to have a seat.

The man got right to the point.

"I need to speak to you confidentially about the Sarah Turner case."

"We promise you that we will be discreet, but if you have information that could help us solve the murder, we will use it. Did you know her?"

"Yes, very well. My company contracted her for almost all of our decorating projects. She was professional and had very good taste. I also bought some works of art from her, and I introduced her to other people who wound up doing business with her. In other words, I helped get her career going. Occasionally I would bring her along with my family to philanthropic events, which were good occasions to meet possible clients."

"So, you were a type of mentor for her, her patron…"

Eric Anderson hesitated.

"Look, I want to be frank with you because I know you're going to find out sooner or later. What you're saying is true… but later on we had an affair… I've never been a womanizer. I love my wife. These things happen."

"You're speaking about the past. Had the relationship ended?"

"Yes… and no. About a month ago, more or less, we mutually decided to call it off… but then something unexpected happened… I went to see her at her apartment at noon on Saturday. I didn't think anything would happen… I didn't go with any intentions, but we made love. I swore it would be the last time. I promise you that when I left she was alive and well."

"We'll have to confirm your story."

"I understand, but I'd like to avoid a scandal. I think my wife suspected something, and I would prefer it if she didn't suffer any humiliation. We've been married for years. She's been such a wonderful partner. She shouldn't pay the price for my mistakes."

"We'll try to be discreet...Anything else?"

Once again, Eric Anderson hesitated. Worse still, he got up to leave. María sensed that he was holding back on some important information.

Just before he headed out, he looked at both of them and said:

"She was six weeks pregnant..."

Chapter 2: The Neighbors

Day 1, Monday

As they had planned to do, the detectives returned to the condominium at 6:00 that evening. Some eight or ten people, almost all women, had gathered and were sitting in the lobby as if they were waiting for them. After they exchanged a glance, Fernández immediately understood what the boss wanted him to do. He approached the group and explained:

"Detective Duquesne and I would be very grateful for your cooperation. We would like to speak with each one of you individually. She will be over in that corner, and I'll sit in the other one. We'll take down your name, which apartment you live in, we'll ask you if you saw something over the weekend, and your general impressions about Sarah Turner. We'd also like you to tell us about any unusual incident in the past that you might have seen. The smallest detail might be important."

The first woman that came up to María was carrying a portable oxygen tank. She had clearly been a beautiful woman, and even at her current age, she still had a look of elegance about her. As soon as

María took down her details, the neighbor began to speak:

"She was an angel. And to think at my age, with two kids and four grandchildren, that hardly anyone ever thinks about this poor old woman! But Sarah on the other hand even took me to the doctor's office, and when she went shopping she would always ask me if I needed anything. I don't like to be a bother, but sometimes I would ask her to pick up some bread or something like that. She was always thinking of others. I never met any of her friends. Even though I live on the same floor, my apartment is down at the other end of the hallway, and I don't get out much, so I can't be certain who tended to visit her. I did however meet her sister once. I think I'm right in telling you she was a good person and that she came from a good family. You can usually tell that sort of thing. It's really a shame…"

The next woman had a somewhat different impression.

"She was a gorgeous woman but a bit of a snob. She barely said hello to me when I ran into her. But, now, with men it was a totally different matter. It doesn't surprise me that something like this happened to her. I don't know what she did for a living… I suspect nothing respectable."

When María asked her if she was aware that she was an interior decorator and art dealer, she was surprised, but then she added with a disparaging tone:

"Appearances can be deceiving … what I mean is, maybe she wasn't what she said she was. I don't know. I didn't care for her."

The third neighbor wasn't any help at all. She only remarked:

"I can't tell you anything. I ran into her in the elevator once. She always seemed to be in a hurry. That's really all I can tell you."

Meanwhile Fernández gathered similar opinions that were of little benefit. One woman described Sarah Turner succinctly:

"She looked very professional. She was always well dressed but distant. She never attended the Condominium Association meetings."

Another was more forthcoming.

"I sell Avon. Sometimes she would buy a few things, although I suspect they weren't for her. I'm sure she used much more expensive beauty products. When I would deliver her order and go to her apartment to collect the payment, she always invited me in. Her apartment was beautiful. Very modern. I prefer more traditional, but regardless I recognize good taste. She was nice… one time when I was out of breath, she insisted that I sit down, and she gave me some water… and didn't let me leave until I was okay."

Finally, one of the neighbors offered some interesting information:

"I live on the same floor, and I'm not a gossip, but sometimes she had men over. That's natural in the case of a beautiful, young woman who's single… No, no I don't know if it was always the same man. Well, about a year or more ago, there was one man who seemed to be her partner, but he had the look of a starving artist… And then a very distinguished gentleman began to come by, but I only saw him a couple of times. And recently, I saw another man that looked like him, but younger. Likewise, she also had female friends who would come by…"

Fernández made a note to bring by a series of photos later on to see if she could identify the visitors. He imagined that the distinguished gentleman was Eric Anderson, but they still had to find the former partner.

The only man in the group was completely frank:

"She was beautiful. I'm an old man, but she was one of those women that regardless of how old you are you can't help but notice her. She was polite, and she didn't make a big stink about it if you looked at her. She ignored it. Believe me, if I had been twenty years younger I would've had a go at it… although I don't know, she had a certain attitude about her of 'look, but don't touch' that would stop anybody in their tracks…"

When they finished the interviews, they went to Betty's apartment. They didn't have to prod her with many questions before she began to speak.

"Yes, Sarah was my best friend. We had arrived in Miami around the same time, both of us from New York. I'm a real estate agent, so we were able to help each other mutually. I would recommend her as an interior decorator and art dealer and, since she had connections with a lot of well-established people, she would let them know when I had some commercial property for sale. Apart from that, we would go out to eat occasionally or to the movies near here in Coral Gables, the one that puts on really good foreign films, or some event at Books and Books, the book store across from the cinema. Have you been there? It's a wonderful place. Sometimes we would eat there, outside in the café on the patio, and enjoy the music that they usually have almost every weekend. Okay, yeah, I guess I should get to the point. Sorry for rambling on. Well, as far as her love life I don't know that much. She was very reserved. Yes, I once met a boyfriend that she had some time ago, a disaster of a young man, a wannabe painter who she got mixed with… but he finally went back to New York… His name was Tim… No, no I don't know his last name but I'm sure it's in her cell… I don't know what else to tell you. I'm in such a state of shock. I have a key to her apartment just like she has one to mine. Look, I can give it back right now, I'd like to get mine back too. I know she kept it in the first cabinet, on the right, in her kitchen. Well, as soon as you can. Don't worry, if I think of anything I'll make sure and call you. You can interview me as many times as you like. I want you to find whoever's guilty. Even though no one can bring my friend back! Do her parents and sister know yet? Yes, they got along well although Sarah didn't say much about her childhood… Well, that's normal. She always looked to the future… She had plans, ambitions… Here's her key… Thank you, and don't forget my keys, they're on a keychain with a little red plastic flashlight."

"Sorry, just one more routine question," Fernández said in a friendly tone, "where were you on Sunday afternoon?"

Betty did not blink.

"I was right here, at home. When Sarah didn't answer my call, I ordered some Chinese food."

"Is there anyone else who could have access to your key to Sarah's apartment?"

"No... Well, as for access, anyone who comes into my apartment, but no one would know that it was her key..."

For the moment, they didn't have any reason to suspect the victim's best friend. Nevertheless, María, who was always thorough and skeptical, told Fernández:

"When you can, only as a precaution, find out what you can about this woman."

It was the doorman who gave them the most important information:

"She was a real lady. She always gave me a great end of year bonus and tipped me well when I helped her with little things. Yes, she had visitors but not many. It's been a long time since that painter with the long hair lived with her. The truth is he wasn't the right fit for such an elegant woman. Her boss, Mr. Anderson, came by every once in a while, always with a briefcase. I guess it was a work thing. Her parents didn't stay with her, but when they were in Miami they always visited. Her sister on the other hand did stay with her occasionally until she got married... I don't know what else to tell you. About last weekend? Well, I think on Saturday during the middle the day Mr. Anderson came by. He wasn't here very long, perhaps an hour or so. And, on Sunday I think I saw her father leave. I didn't see him come in... And he didn't answer me when I called out his name to say hello and also to see if he needed a taxi. He just kept on walking in a hurry… Maybe it wasn't him, because it seemed like he was limping, and Mr. Turner doesn't have a limp. But he was wearing a raincoat just like the one he always wears. Come to think of it, it's odd because it was really hot outside. It is true that it looked like it was going to rain… It's probably just a thing with people from New York."

Chapter 3: The Family

Days 1 and 2, Monday and Tuesday

As they were leaving the building, María received a text from Colleen Turner Maxwell to let her know that she was with her parents in the Biltmore Hotel and to ask if they could meet up the next morning. María answered saying that she would come by to pick them up at 9:30, to which she immediately received a positive reply.

María and Fernández went to Seasons 52 on Miracle Mile, just a few blocks away from the crime scene. They each ordered a glass of wine and something light to eat. María was hoping to get the initial results from the autopsy and let the forensic doctor know that she would bring the family by in the morning to identify the body. She sent a text to Dr. John Erwin, which he answered a few minutes later. Yes, she could bring the family by after 10:00. The preliminary report listed the cause of death as blunt trauma to the head, and also indicated that Sarah Turner was indeed pregnant. As for the rest of the analysis, they would still have to wait a bit longer for the other test results, such as blood alcohol level and the toxicology report.

27

The detectives knew it was early in the investigation to make any type of conjecture. They had to find out more about Eric Anderson. They couldn't discard him just because he had come to see them and had come clean about his affair with the young woman. It could be a type of deception through truth, when you confess that you're guilty of smaller things so that your honesty makes you seem innocent of the murder, something much worse than having had an affair. And obviously, it was important to find out if he was the father of her unborn child. They would also have to verify if Sarah's father came to see her on Sunday as the doorman had indicated, but that seemed unlikely since he was in New York when they called to relay the news. Well, actually, they couldn't be sure where he was since María had only spoken with the sister. It was always a necessary but delicate task to rule out family members.

While they waited for their food, María searched for information on Eric Anderson. She found out that *Forbes* magazine had included him on their list of the top four-hundred wealthiest individuals in the United States and, among those, the highest-ranking real estate agent. They estimated his net worth to be more than fifteen billion dollars. His parents, who were from a modest background, had divorced when he was young. He studied business administration and economics at the University of Washington. After serving two years in the Marine Corps, he built his first house in Newport Beach, California in 1958. That year he founded a company with two partners, and they bought 10,000 acres of land for urban development. Despite some setbacks related to the country's economic cycles, his career was an exemplary model of the man who starts with nothing and climbs his way to the top. Mrs. Anderson, on the other hand, came from a well-to-do New England family.

María put down her reading when the food arrived. She suddenly realized how hungry she was. She didn't even answer the phone when her father called and instead promised herself that she would call him back on her way home.

They were not quite full, so they ordered a decaf and some small pastries that they served at that particular restaurant, perfect for finishing off one's dinner with something sweet without feeling guilty for the amount of calories consumed. While they were waiting for dessert, the detectives researched the victim's family whom they would meet the next morning. Mr. Ralph Turner was a radiologist at Mount Sinai Hospital in New York; her mother, Joy, was a relatively successful painter. Her sister, Colleen, had been married for two years to a stockbroker and had a one-year-old boy. Sarah had graduated from The Columbia School of Visual Arts and had worked for several years as a curator in a small museum. Later on, she took a few courses in interior decorating until she began a change of career with Timothy Parker as her partner. A few months after starting the company, Sarah moved to Miami at the beginning of 2013. No one in the Anderson or Turner family had any criminal record.

The next morning María mentally went over the information she had learned as she headed to meet Sarah's family at the Biltmore Hotel, one of the city's historical and architectural landmarks. María loved that place. When her friends visited Miami, she took so many of them there that she knew its history well, such as how it had been the tallest building in Florida when it was constructed in 1926. More importantly, that is where the rich and famous stayed, and it had become a center of fashion and sports, especially for swim meets due to its enormous swimming pool. Throughout its hallways one could still see black and white photos of its famous guests, such as the Duke and Duchess of Windsor and even President Franklin D. Roosevelt. During World War II, the hotel had been converted into a hospital. Later on, it fell into disrepair until its reopening in 1983. The Biltmore had a magnificent restaurant, even though what really interested María was its architecture, which according to what she had read, had been inspired by the Giralda in Seville. Her parents always said that it looked just like the Hotel Nacional in Havana.

After meeting the Turners in the lobby, María suggested that they confer before going to identify the body since it was a painful experience and they might prefer to be alone afterwards, but the mother insisted:

"Look, it's just that until I see my daughter, I'm not going to be able to believe that this has really happened."

María knew the protocol well: accompany the family to the morgue, ask them to take a seat in the waiting room, use the intercom to let them know when to bring the body to the large window, ask the next of kin if they were ready, and then observe their reactions of surprise, pain, confusion, rage, or controlled emotions. Some insisted on going in and caressing the hair of their loved one. Others preferred to leave the window as soon as possible, closing their eyes in order to avoid seeing the gaze of death on their loved one's face.

The Turners' reaction was calm. The mother cried silently, gasping in sobs that seemed to flow inwardly and embitter the soul; the father closed his lips tightly and blinked repeatedly, as if holding back the tears.

31

The sister hugged the two of them as she cried. She kept saying:

"Why? Why?"

The Turners agreed to go down to headquarters to continue their conversation even though Duquesne offered to do it in the hotel.

"Do you know of anyone who could want to harm her?"

It was the mother, still calm, who answered:

"Actually, no, but you should find out where her ex-husband, Tim Parker, was."

María was surprised that she hadn't known until that moment that Sarah had been married.

"He's a painter without any talent whatsoever. I always told Sarah, but he can be such a charmer. They met when she worked in the museum. They got married down at the courthouse, without telling a soul. I think she knew we wouldn't approve. I don't know what my daughter was thinking. They could have just lived together without getting married. In the end, they started a business together, and it didn't last a year because not only did he never do his share of the work, but he even stole from the company. She realized what happened, shut everything down, filed for divorce, and moved to Miami."

"He had the nerve to refuse to sign the papers," interrupted Colleen. "He followed her to Miami. At some point, they got back together, but she stood her ground, and she finally kicked him out of her house. I, for one, haven't heard anything about him since then, and their divorce was final about two years ago."

"Did she demand that he return the money that he had stolen?" asked María.

"No, she didn't think it was worth it, and that it would be a long, drawn-out process. She preferred just to forget about it and not see him again. He was broke, and she wasn't going to get the money back anyway. She only took him to court for the divorce."

"Do you know how we could find him?"

"If you called the galleries in Soho, I think somebody could probably tell you since he was a painter, even though a bad one," suggested Joy.

"Was he ever violent towards her? Do you think he was capable of having killed her?"

"He never hit her, at least as far as we know," now it was the father who was speaking, "but when he drank he got aggressive. Capable of murder? I guess we all are… In a fit of rage anything could happen."

María took advantage of the moment and gingerly asked:

"I'm sorry, these are very delicate questions, but I'm obliged to ask you. Where were each one of you on Sunday from five o'clock in the evening to eight that night?"

"Me? I was home with my husband and son, and also the neighbors who had come over for a cup of coffee. You can check with them if you want," explained the sister immediately without being offended by the question.

"I was at Peter Lik's gallery in Soho. I had taken some of my paintings by, and then we went for a glass of wine at a bar nearby. I can give you his number, and you can verify it."

It seemed to María that the father was thinking about his answer.

"I was at the home alone, and then later I went to work, but I fell asleep waiting for a patient who was coming to the Emergency Room but never arrived. I didn't get back home until the next morning, just a little bit before you called with the terrible news."

Later on María would have time to confirm their alibis, especially the father's which seemed a bit shaky. Right now, however, she wanted to concentrate on obtaining more information about Sarah.

"What do you know about her life in Miami? Was she happy?"

The three of them agreed that she worked a lot but seemed to be happy.

"The last time I saw her was less than two weeks ago. She invited me to the grand opening of an office that she had decorated and where she had used some of my paintings. She was radiant, prettier than ever, I don't know, like she had a special glow about her."

"Did you know that she was pregnant?"

The surprise on the parent's face was genuine. The sister's silence however led María to think that maybe she knew more, but she preferred to ask her later in private.

Next, she asked them about Sarah's relationship with the Andersons. The young woman's parents had nothing but praise, such as how they had helped her so much, how all the Andersons took care of her, how they had become her other family and so on... all of which helped them feel more at ease knowing that she wasn't alone in the city.

As soon as María heard Fernández coming down the hallway, she immediately called him in. After making presentations, she asked him to accompany the parents to the other room so they could sign the necessary papers in order to release the body once they had finished the autopsy.

"Offer them a coffee or whatever they might like…" That was María's way of getting her partner to slow things down a bit so she could have more time to talk with Colleen.

She got right to the point.

"You knew that she was expecting?"

"Yes, she called me crying two weeks ago to tell me."

"And do you know who the father is?"

"I have my suspicions, but given the seriousness of the matter I wouldn't dare speculate. Couldn't you find out with a DNA test?"

"Yes, but we would need the DNA of the suspected father to verify it."

"I don't think that she had told him, so he wouldn't have a motive…"

"But what if she did end up telling him?"

"She would've told me. We spoke daily. Besides, I think, in fact I'm almost certain, that she had decided to get an abortion. Last Sunday, she called me and I didn't answer the phone because I was in the shower. And then, I didn't call her back! I didn't answer the last call from my sister… I failed her…"

The young woman covered her face with her hands and broke down in tears.

María waited a few moments until she could pull herself together.

"Look, Colleen, you're going to feel much better if you help us catch whoever did this to your sister. Who do you think the baby's father was?"

The young woman sighed deeply and said in a shaky voice:

"Eric…"

"Eric Anderson?"

"Yes, Junior, the son."

Chapter 4: Linda Astor Anderson

Day 3, Wednesday

Fernández found out everything he could about the Andersons just as his boss had asked. As soon as she arrived at headquarters, he told her:

"I haven't had time to write up the report yet, but I can tell you what I've found out. The Andersons have three kids. The oldest is Elizabeth, thirty-six years old. She has a position on the Board of Directors of her family's company, but she doesn't work there. She's a real estate agent. She's been married for seven years to Rick Moreno, originally from Colombia, and who's been relatively successful as a banker. They have two young daughters. They live in Cocoplum. Neither one of them has a criminal record. Between the two of them, they bring in around $300,000 a year."

"Do you know if they had any type of relationship with Sarah Turner?"

"They show up together in a few group photos taken at fundraising events for charities, and Sarah appears as the official decorator at some of the properties sold by Elizabeth. I don't know if they had any type of personal relationship."

"And the two sons?"

"Eric is thirty-four years old, a graduate of Harvard and the Wharton School of Business. Oh, and I forgot to tell you, Elizabeth studied architecture here, at the University of Miami. Eric Jr. got married very young, when he was at Harvard. The marriage only lasted a year and a half. He had a son who's now around thirteen and lives with his mom in Naples. He remarried two years ago, and they just had a baby girl a few weeks ago. They live in Coral Gables. He works with his father as an executive in his company."

"And the younger one?"

"Marty is twenty-eight. He graduated from Berkeley. He lives with his partner, Yoel, in Coconut Grove."

"So he's gay?"

"Yes," Fernández answered with a slight grin since he was too and he didn't try to hide it.

"And a musician, although up until now he hasn't been too successful. He doesn't work for the firm in any capacity."

"What can you tell me about the mother?"

"Linda Astor Anderson comes from one of the richest families in the country. The Waldorf-Astoria and even the Astoria neighborhood in Queens is named after them. She was born and raised in New York. A true aristocrat, but she's not dumb. She graduated *summa cum laude* from Wellesley College. She's very active philanthropically. She is sixty-years old, elegant, and very attractive. She lives with her husband in a penthouse on Brickell Avenue. She appears to have a position in his firm, but it doesn't look like she meddles in the business."

María thought for a moment.

"Which one do you want to interview first?" Fernández asked.

"The *grande dame*, and try to make the appointment for today, as soon as possible, and I want you to come with me."

Two hours later Duquesne and Fernández were in the lobby of the elegant building on Brickell Avenue. After Mrs. Anderson's buzzed them in, they took the elevator directly to the only apartment on the top floor.

She opened the door herself and just as Fernández had described her, everything about her reflected her high social class. She had on a simple black dress, a pearl necklace, bracelets, earrings, and rings that clearly were not costume jewelry.

As she walked in front of them on their way to the living room, Fernández whispered to María:

"Rickie."

He realized that she did not understand that Rickie Freeman was the designer of the dress and that it costs several hundred dollars, so he mumbled that he would explain later.

María tried not to let on how impressed she was by the luxury of the apartment. She couldn't stop thinking about how different it was from Sarah Turner's, which was so modern. Although both of them were of top quality and in good taste, this one was decorated with high-end furniture and antiques.

Mrs. Anderson accompanied them to a sitting room with large windows that offered a spectacular view of the bay and bridge that connected to Key Biscayne. They had barely sat down when a maid appeared dressed in a uniform, something María had never seen before in Miami or anywhere for that matter. They accepted an iced tea.

"So, how can I help you?" said the woman addressing them.

"*She's taking the first step, wanting to control the interview*," María thought. She took out her tape recorder and, rather than asking for permission, simply asserted:

"We need to record the conversation." Linda Anderson didn't seem fazed. "What can you tell us about Sarah Turner?"

"The poor dear. What happened to her was such a shame. How are her parents? Do you have any leads yet on who it was?"

"Excuse me, Mrs. Anderson, but we're the ones asking the questions. Tell us what you know about her."

The woman made a gesture with her mouth that let María know that she wasn't accustomed to someone talking to her like that, but she composed herself and answered calmly.

"We met her shortly after she arrived in Miami from New York, some two or three years ago. I think a mutual friend recommended her to Eric. She decorated quite a few of the lobbies in the firm's various buildings, and also some model homes in the suburbs that my daughter oversees and for which she serves as the broker. She was always very professional. She has exquisite taste. Well, she *had*… It's so difficult to talk about her in the past."

"What was your family's relationship like with her?"

"Very cordial. She would often go to charity events that we were involved in. She was always good company. One knew that she would carry herself as a real lady, never too much to drink, never a controversial comment."

"Did she have a closer relationship with either your husband or with your son?"

"Naturally since she worked directly with them, as well as my daughter, she saw them more often than I."

"Is that all?"

"I don't know what you're insinuating, and besides you'd have to ask them, wouldn't you?"

She was clearly displeased now. She sat on the edge of her seat as if she were about to stand up and end in the conversation.

"One more moment, please." It was Fernández who intervened this time. "Sorry, but it's a routine question. Where were you Saturday evening?"

"With my husband at a fundraising dinner for the Florida Grand Opera," answered Mrs. Anderson with an air of superiority.

"And I imagine that you probably spent Sunday at home resting," Fernández replied kindly.

"Yes, I was here all day and night. I had had an exhausting week."

"And your husband?" This time it was María who asked.

"He went to play golf and have a few drinks with his friends. You can ask them at the Club. Later we had dinner here."

The detectives got to their feet and thanked the aristocrat for her cooperation. She seemed relieved and anxious for them to leave. María wanted to intimidate her a bit. She paused at the elevator door, offered her card, and told her to call if she remembered anything else. And then she added:

"What a lovely apartment you have. Did Sarah Turner decorate it?"

Right then the elevator arrived and Mrs. Anderson almost pushed them inside. She didn't answer the question.

"You're bad, María," Fernández chided her with a smile.

"Seriously. What do you think?"

"I'm not sure."

"Let's get back to the office and take a look at the coverage of the security cameras for the entrances and exits of the parking garage, and then you head over to the Club to confirm that Eric Anderson was indeed there on Sunday and for how long. We'll know soon if they are telling the truth.

Chapter 5: Junior

Day 3, Wednesday

Once back at headquarters, the detectives reviewed the tapes they had finally acquired of the lobby and the entranceway from the building's garage on Biltmore Way where the murder had taken place, as well as those from the parking garage of the condominium where Eric Anderson and his wife lived.

It took them hours. In the first ones, they in fact saw Anderson arrive at Biltmore Way at noon on Saturday with a briefcase in his hand and then take off with his head down one hour and fifteen minutes later. It surprised them to see Junior come in and leave all within thirty minutes on Sunday morning. They also saw another person leave around 7:00 at night, someone in a raincoat with a limp just as the doorman had described. Regardless of their efforts to go over and over the tapes, they never saw him enter. Likewise, the camera never got a good look at his face. It was as if he knew how to avoid it. There was a moment, a little before, when a large group entered and someone might have come in without being readily noticed. Obviously, there was also the possibility of entering through the garage and coming in through the back door, but that would require an access key that usually only the tenants or employees had.

On the tapes that showed the back entrance, they saw various tenants come and go. In a few instances, it seemed like the tape went dark, as if someone had covered up the camera lens. At other times, they thought they saw some type of shadow that they could barely make out. They paused and rewound the tape several times but, in the end, they couldn't draw any firm conclusions.

"If we have to, we may need to hand these tapes over to the experts," María said.

On the Brickell Avenue tapes, they observed Anderson arrive at the garage on Saturday afternoon, and then the elegantly dressed couple left at 7:00 that evening before returning at 11:30. On Sunday, he left at 4:00 in the afternoon and returned three hours later.

María decided to let Fernández go to the Club by himself and confirm the exact hours when Anderson had been there on Sunday while she focused on the appointment with Eric Jr.

The young man was pleasant on the phone, but there was something in his voice that made María think he was nervous. She gave him the choice of either coming down to headquarters or she could go by his office or home. Junior preferred the former, which led the detective to believe that the young millionaire preferred to keep the matter as private as possible. She put a large question mark by his name.

When she heard her phone ring and saw on the screen that it was her father, she remembered that she hadn't returned any of his previous calls.

"I'm sorry dad," she said in her most apologetic tone.

"Don't worry *mija*. I know you must be busy with the Biltmore Way case.

"How'd you know?"

"They're talking about it on TV, and they're calling it 'Murder on Biltmore Way.'"

"Jeez, the press loves to put labels on things these days."

"I just wanted to make sure you were okay, and to see if you needed anything or if I could help at all."

"Have you spoken to Patrick?"

"Yeah, just yesterday. Your son's fine, studying, working, dating."

"What? Does he have a girlfriend?"

"No, not that I know of. It's just a way of saying he's always going out with girls."

"Oh, okay," María sighed with relief.

"Look, *Papi*, I have to get ready for an interview. I promise you as soon as I can, I'll come by. Take care."

"You too, *mija*."

When Eric arrived, María had him come in to one of the interrogation rooms and deliberately made him wait for over ten minutes. At first, he sat there calmly with his arms crossed on his chest, but then he began to check his watch every fifteen seconds. Finally, he started pacing back and forth in the small room at least a dozen times. When it looked like he was about to open the door, María came in. Surprised, the man jumped back a little.

"Sorry that you had to wait. Have a seat please. Can we get you some water, a coffee, a cold drink?"

"No thank you. I'm in a bit of a rush."

"If you prefer, we can reschedule for another time. I can come by your house or your office, as I mentioned earlier. It's a matter of routine."

Junior seemed to relax a bit and sat back in his chair. María noticed how strikingly similar he looked to his father, except the son was perhaps a bit shorter and, obviously, wasn't graying in his temples.

"I was hoping you could tell me what Sarah Turner was like," María began.

"She did her job well. She was a great decorator and art connoisseur, especially of modern art. She was very professional, serious, and punctual. She worked well under pressure. There was nothing that seemed to perturb her."

"She was also very beautiful."

"Yes," answered Eric Jr. with perhaps a touch of irony in his voice, "and even though it isn't fair, in some lines of work one's good looks can be an asset."

"And, beyond your professional relationship, was she a friend of the family?"

"Well, I don't know if you'd really call it a friendship. A lot of times my father took her along to dinners for charity events. He would pay for an entire table and he needed to fill it. Sarah always knew how to carry herself, and for my mother that was very important. Obviously, she also always attended the company's Christmas parties, and sometimes she'd be at some reception or dinner at my parents' house."

"How did she get along with your sister?"

Junior took a deep breath.

"On the surface of things, fine. Sarah decorated some of the model homes that Elizabeth had designed and later sold. But my sister can be difficult. Between you and me, I think she was a little jealous of Sarah, maybe it was a female thing because she was so beautiful or maybe she resented not working directly with us in the firm. She brings that up each chance she gets, that she's the oldest but that I was always Dad's favorite since I'm a man. She's also convinced that Mom doesn't approve of her husband because he's Hispanic. And maybe she's right. Mom couldn't be a bigger WASP," Junior smiled as if he had done something bad. Duquesne was pleased that he was relaxing a bit.

"Can you think of anyone who would want to harm her?"

"No, a long time ago she was involved with a guy who was really sketchy, but as far as I know they ended it, and he no longer lives here."

"What was the nature of the relationship between your father and her?"

"As I said already, she did a lot of work for our firm."

María took note that Junior seemed defensive.

"And when was the last time you saw her?"

"I think at the office on Friday morning."

María knew he was lying.

"And what was your relationship like with her?"

"I've already explained that to you."

"I'm sorry, Mr. Anderson, but I don't think you've been totally honest with me."

Clearly irritated, the man got to his feet.

María ordered him with a stern voice: "Sit down." And he obeyed.

"Look, we have video from the building where Sarah lived, and we know you went to visit her Sunday morning."

Eric Jr. reacted immediately.

"Oh yeah, you're right, I had completely forgotten that. I went over to take her appointment book because she had left it at the office, and she asked me to run it by. That was the only free moment I had before heading to the Club. I was just there a moment. But believe me, she was perfectly fine."

"Have you forgotten anything else?"

"No, no I don't think so," Junior answered with a bit of uncertainty in his voice.

"Were you at the Club all afternoon?"

"Yes, until about 7:00 that night. I played golf with my father. You can ask him."

"We'll inquire with the Club. And it's best if you don't leave the city for a few days since we may have more questions we would like to ask."

Eric seemed to have recovered his composure or at least he knew how to fake it.

"Don't worry. I wouldn't even think about not being with Sarah's family at a time like this."

María thought she detected a real or maybe even feigned sadness in him brought about by the death of a close friend or, who knows, perhaps even a lover.

Chapter 6: The Funeral

Days 3 and 4, Wednesday and Thursday

María was going over her notes from the interview with Eric Anderson Jr. when Fernández returned to headquarters. They immediately conferred.

"Well, the Andersons's alibis seem to check out. The son got to the Club at 12:00 when he had lunch with some friends and then he played golf with his father. The two of them left at 6:40 p.m. in separate cars. The golf course is a few blocks from Sarah's apartment. We saw the father enter his building on Brickell at 7:05 p.m., so I think we can discard him, but we don't know what time Junior got back home. We didn't see him enter or leave Biltmore Way, but that person wearing the rain coat, the one who was limping, seems very suspicious to me. Maybe he came in without the camera seeing him, maybe at the same time a large group with suitcases was arriving or something like that?"

"Yes, and besides he lied to me during the interrogation, and I have an idea that he's hiding a lot more things."

"On a different note, the alibis check out for Sarah's mother and sister. No one remembers having seen her father at the hospital, but what reason could there possibly be for a father to murder his daughter? Although in the moment of a heated discussion, anyone could accidentally deliver a blow that they shouldn't have. I've looked into all the roundtrip flights from New York to Miami. His name doesn't appear on any of the manifests, but he had time to get here and return. I wouldn't discard Mr. Turner just yet. Maybe she told him she was expecting and he went ballistic."

"We won't eliminate him yet, but that family doesn't seem like it would react like that, and even more so given how old Sarah was. If it were him, there would have to be another motive."

"What would help us the most is to know who's the father."

"Yes, but the Andersons have good lawyers, and they're not going to offer their DNA voluntarily, and we still don't have enough evidence to ask for a court order to make them do it."

María received a call from Colleen. There was not going to be a viewing, but they were going to have a church service the next day at 11:00 a.m. at the Coral Gables Congregational Church. The body would then be cremated. Her parents would have preferred to bury her in New York, but Sarah left detailed instructions in writing. She wanted her ashes to be sprinkled in the ocean. Her sister told the detective that she shouldn't feel obliged to attend the service but, if she wanted to, that the family would be very grateful.

As soon as they hung up, María called Dr. Erwin. She wanted to make sure that before they handed over the body that they had everything they needed from the mother and fetus in order to run a paternity test. With his customary patience and professionalism, the forensic doctor assured her that everything was in order. He explained that in addition to the blow to the head, which had been the cause of death, there was also a hematoma on the back of the skull and that there was a suspicious amount of benzodiazepine in her blood. In the end, he was able to confirm Sarah's pregnancy: she was seven weeks along. María remembered that Mr. Anderson had said six. Could the difference be of some importance? And why was a pregnant woman taking Xanax or something similar?

Located directly across from the Biltmore Hotel, the church was well known not only for its stunning Colonial Spanish architecture but also as a popular wedding venue. Divorcees often chose to get remarried there since they weren't required to seek an annulment, which the Catholic Church demanded. María had attended more than one wedding at the church. One Miami celebrity had gotten married there with his second and third wife with less than two years in between the ceremonies. She had also spoken on several occasions with its Pastor, a young Cuban American who came from a family of intellectuals and diplomats back in Cuba, and who always included great sensitivity, common sense, and the right amount of humor in his sermons. She didn't recall ever having attended a funeral there.

Duquesne and Fernández arrived early. She discreetly stood to one side of the main entrance, and he at the side door. They wanted to see who was attending and how they acted. Moreover, both of them were wearing a small camera attached to their wrists in case they felt like they needed to take any photos. They agreed to do so only if they saw someone they couldn't identify or if somebody was behaving suspiciously.

At 10:40 a.m. there was still no one there; but a few minutes later, as if they had all agreed to a set time, everyone began to arrive at the same moment. María watched Eric Anderson climb out of his dark Lexus. It seemed odd that his wife wasn't with him, but barely a few seconds later she parked her BMW beside her husband's car and they both walked into the church together. It didn't go unnoticed by the detective that they had kept a prudent distance between each other, maintaining a sufficient space on the one hand that didn't run the risk of even touching one another but at the same time not so much space that others might suspect some type of aloofness between them. For his part, Fernández recognized several of Sarah's neighbors including her best friend Betty.

Junior guided his wife Laura along by her arm, a gesture María interpreted as his need for control. It looked like she was still carrying around those extra pounds in her waist that are sometimes difficult for women to lose after a pregnancy. Elizabeth, the Anderson's daughter, also arrived in a separate car from her husband Rick Moreno. She didn't seem to have her mother's aristocratic air nor her brother's petulance. She came off simply as a typical mother of a family—a soccer mom—despite wearing a dark dress with an elegant cut. Moreno fit the Latin stereotype perfectly. He was wearing a white *guayabera* and trousers along with dark sunglasses that he never took off for a second, even during the religious ceremony itself. Marty, the youngest of the Anderson's kids, came with his partner without calling attention to their amorous relationship but not trying to hide it either, although María wondered if she didn't perceive it that way since she already knew about them beforehand. Without knowing that, she might have presumed they were simply colleagues from work. She also made a mental note to find out if they were legally married and to check out any pre-nuptial agreements that the Anderson's sons and daughter might have. Money was always the most common motive in crimes, and if there was going to be one more offspring who would get a share of the inheritance, each and every one of them could have wished for it not to be born.

The Turners arrived in a limousine provided by the funeral home. They seemed to be more fragile than when she had met them earlier, as if the three of them had suddenly aged in just a few hours. Colleen's husband also accompanied them.

There was a tense moment when they brought out the casket. It obviously hadn't occurred to the Turners that they would need eight men to carry it and lift it up the stairs of the church. Her father, Sarah's brother-in-law, Eric Anderson, and his son Junior immediately came forward when the funeral director gave them a nod, but they still needed four more volunteers. It didn't surprise María when Colleen joined them. She had read that women could be pallbearers, but she had never seen one. Colleen grabbed one of the casket's handles with such force that she knew no one was going to separate her from her dead sister, much less in that particular church that customarily allowed and emboldened practices beyond traditional ones. She watched the Pastor proceed from the altar along the rows of dark wood benches, as he seemed to be looking for others to whom he could give a nod to help bring in the casket. Marty immediately got to his feet, followed by his partner, and joined the funeral procession. Fernández was just about to do the same when he saw an elderly gentleman walking slowly toward the door. It was Sarah's neighbor, the one who had said that if he had been twenty years younger, he would have tried to win her love.

Before he could make his way to the casket, however, without knowing exactly from where he had appeared, a well-dressed man in a gray suit and long hair pulled back in a ponytail took his place in the eighth and final spot. María saw how Mr. Turner and Colleen shot him a reproachful scowl, to which he answered in a low voice:

"She was my wife, and we loved each other."

Everything had transpired in just a few minutes, but for those who were conscious of the situation, it had seemed like an eternity.

The ceremony was brief and included elegant and somber music selected by the family. The only crying that could be heard came from one of the side benches. María was finally able to see the woman who was sobbing. It was Aura, the Nicaraguan woman who cleaned Miss Turner's apartment once a week, and who had discovered her body just four days ago.

Chapter 7: Elizabeth

Day 5, Friday

The day after the funeral, María asked Fernández to set up an appointment with Elizabeth, the oldest of Anderson's children, and to assure her that they just needed to go over some routine questions. She willingly agreed to do so, but asked if they could meet at her house.

The last time María had been in Cocoplum she thought it looked like a community made up of nouveaux riches. Even though it didn't have the elegance of Coral Gables, over the years it had taken on its own character. The expensive and well-built residencies didn't have that cookie-cutter type look to them since the owners had put their own personal touches on their houses. Likewise, the vegetation had taken off. The community had its own parks, clubs, canals, and even a marina for yachts.

Elizabeth and Rick Moreno's house had high gables with large windows that allowed generous portions of sunlight, as well as a view of their large pool and terrace in the backyard. The house was tastefully decorated and showed small signs of disarray often apparent in homes with small children. A pair of tennis shoes in the corner, schoolbooks on the kitchen table, a few cushions out of place. Elizabeth herself came to the door and invited them in to an informal den adjacent to the kitchen where she could watch the kids play out in the backyard.

"What can I do for you?"

"Just some routine questions," María answered while she turned on her tape recorder.

"We have to record all the interviews," she explained, as if excusing herself, "but if there is something confidential that we need to talk about, we can turn it off."

"No, that won't be necessary."

"What can you tell us about Sarah Turner?"

"I guess my family will have already mentioned it, but she was very efficient, discreet, and beautiful. She had good taste and class. In short, a real treasure."

María noticed a certain hint of irony or contempt in her tone. She went right to the point.

"But you didn't care for her, right?"

"What wasn't to like?"

Fernández interrupted: "Personally I wouldn't like it if my father and brother placed such high importance on a woman in the family business that

I'm not even a part of, especially when I'm the eldest."

Elizabeth jumped up rather quickly and stuck her head out into the patio to tell the kids to be more careful.

María thought that she had done so to stall. Even then, when she sat back down, she hesitated before speaking.

"Look, it's a long story, and Sarah doesn't have anything to do with it. Junior has always been my father's favorite. Because I'm a woman and Marty has his 'issues,' he's always treated us two differently. Not when it comes to our personal relationship—he's very affectionate—but in business matters. I've accepted that's the way it is. They say that Latin men are very chauvinistic, but so are Americans although they hide it better. My father is more that way than my husband, maybe because they belong to different generations."

"How did you get along with Sarah?"

"Professionally, very well. As for our personal relationship, I wouldn't say that we were really friends."

"She wouldn't have shared any personal problem with you?"

"No, and I wouldn't have confided in her either. Why? Are you aware of something?"

"She was expecting, and we believe that the father was a married man."

Elizabeth went pale.

"And you think it was someone from my family? I assure you my husband would never..."

"We don't suspect your husband."

"Then, my brother?"

"We don't know. What do you think?"

"Well, now that you mention it, I think there could have been something between her and Junior."

"Why do you say that?"

"Do you mind turning off the tape recorder?"

"Of course."

"Look, I don't want to cause problems for my brother, but occasionally when she would hand my brother a drink, their fingers perhaps lingered longer than they needed to, or when we would take a photo he would put his arm tightly around her waist, or they would exchange glances, you know, with that secret language that couples who are in love have or the ones who are caught up in a forbidden love. Does that make sense?"

"Yes, it does. Is there anything else you can tell us?"

"No, well... my sister-in-law was very jealous of her, and it wasn't for nothing because women have a sense about these things."

"And your father?"

"My father? He's only interested in business dealings. I don't think he would have noticed."

"What I mean is do you think he could have been involved in an intimate relationship with Sarah?"

"Oh my God, no! He's a very serious man, and he's always been faithful to my mother."

There was an awkward silence. Elizabeth asked out loud as if she were addressing the questions to herself and not to the detectives:

"And what if Sarah Turner tried to seduce them and to have a child with either one of them in order to lay claim to part of my father's fortune?"

María waited a few seconds and turned the tape recorder back on:

"Sorry, but one more routine question. Where were you on Sunday afternoon?"

"Let's see... oh... I took the kids to a birthday party, here in the neighborhood. I can give you their phone number. Rick was there also. We're friends with a lot of our neighbors."

On the way back to the station, María mentioned to Fernández:

"She's really smart and raised the same question we did. It's not important who seduced whom, but the murderer's motive certainly could have been to keep Sarah's child from having a claim to any part of the Anderson's fortune, not to mention a way of avoiding the scandal too."

Chapter 8: Marty

Day 5, Friday

The Anderson's youngest son lived with his partner in a beautiful house in Coconut Grove. Once there Fernández gushed over the large windows, the floors, and other decorations, to which the young man responded with false modesty:

"My husband and I make our living this way. We buy old houses in disrepair, and we fix them up, live in them a while, and then sell them for a considerable profit."

"So, you two have been together for a while?"

"Yes, together for eight years and married for three." It was amusing to María that eight years seemed like a long time to him.

Once everyone had taken a seat, Duquesne turned on her tape recorder and reminded the young man that the interview was standard procedure. She then asked him the same questions in the same order as all the others and received the same answers: Sarah was an excellent professional; the family appreciated her very much; and it was unbelievable what had happened to her. He told them that he and Yoel had stayed at home on Sunday night. They could confirm that with his husband, but he understood that the word of his spouse would probably not be enough. He didn't know how else to corroborate it.

"Don't worry. For the moment we don't have you on the list of suspects."

"But should we?" asked Fernández.

"Are you asking if I killed Sarah? My goodness, I can't even kill a little lizard. I shoo them out on to the patio. Besides, what motive would I possibly have?" he asked almost laughing.

"To keep there from being yet another heir to the family fortune."

Marty seemed genuinely intrigued.

María spoke slowly so she could measure the impact that each word had on the young man.

"Sarah was pregnant, and we believe the baby's father was perhaps a member of your family."

"I can understand why you don't consider me a suspect, because you're not going to think I'm the father, but maybe I'm the uncle."

"Why do you say that? Do you think there was something between her and your brother?"

"My brother has always been a womanizer, and even though he says that he's settled down ever since he got remarried, I don't believe it."

"Is there any reason why you think that he was having an affair with Sarah?"

Marty thought for a moment. He went to the bar and offered them something to drink. The detectives declined his offer, and their host served himself a glass of champagne.

Wow, champagne at 2:00 in the afternoon, thought Duquesne who wasn't used to visiting people with this type of lifestyle. The criminal world tended to be much less sophisticated.

"Yes, Junior and Sarah were lovers, and he killed her."

Fernández and Duquesne remained silent, waiting for him to continue. Marty let out a loud laugh.

"Don't you see that if he's guilty, my father might have to actually look me in the face?"

María was increasingly becoming aware of the severe level of tension among the Andersons.

"He doesn't accept that you're gay?" Fernández asked, addressing him in a familiar tone.

"He doesn't even acknowledge it. I've never gotten the chance to talk to him about it. And it's as if

Yoel were invisible. My father has never been in our house, and it's not because we haven't invited him."

"And the rest of the family?"

"My brother's the same, even though we sometimes go out to lunch. My sister Elizabeth is a sweetheart and gets along swimmingly with Yoel. We've even gone over to babysit her girls a few times."

"And Mrs. Anderson?" María wanted to know.

"My mother is a great lady. She loves me, and accepts who I am, but in her own way. It's strange. She always seems to be above everything, even though deep down she frets over what people might think or say. She's numb to gossip, but I assume you haven't come to talk me about my personal problems with my family. I don't know how else I can help you."

"Can I ask you a personal question? Did you and Yoel sign a pre-nup? Did your father ask each one of you to sign one before getting married?"

"He never asked me for anything. I'm sure he never thought I could get married. And, to tell you the truth, he doesn't know we're married. And even if he did, I couldn't offend my partner by asking such a thing. If I die, he can inherit my portion. He deserves it for putting up with me," he said with the same chuckle as before.

"Sorry, just out of curiosity, where did you meet Yoel? What does he do for a living? He's Cuban, right?" Fernández casually asked as if they were friends.

"You can tell he's Cuban by the way he dresses, and even more so when he speaks! He still has an accent even though he came over when he was fourteen. He works at a gym. Haven't you noticed how built he is."

María got up to leave, but her partner continued the conversation.

"And how's your music coming?"

"Wow, you can tell you're detectives because no one in the world knows me as a musician, at least not yet. You never know when I might just surprise everyone."

They said goodbye at the door in a friendly way.

Once back in the car, María looked at Fernández, but before she could speak, he interrupted, saying:

"I know. I should find out everything I can about Yoel. I'm already on it. His surname is Nuñez and his given name is a combination of his parents' names: Yolanda and Eladio. He came from Cuba ten years ago on a raft, and got his citizenship with the help of Marty's lawyers, but he hasn't registered to vote. I haven't had time to see if he has a criminal record."

María was more and more grateful for her partner's adeptness.

71

Chapter 9: Crocodiles

Day 6, Saturday

María didn't have any illusions about not working over the weekend, but she had at least hoped to sleep in on Saturday for a bit. The phone woke her at 8:00 in the morning. It was her boss asking her to come to headquarters that morning.

"Is it urgent? Something about the Sarah Turner case?"

"It's not urgent, and it's not about the Turner case, but I need you to come in. We arrested Daniel Gomez's son yesterday," Lawrence Keppler told her in his booming voice.

While she took a shower, María went over the case mentally. Daniel Gomez, along with his two accomplices, had brutally murdered his partner some seven years ago. Gomez and the victim were under investigation for a case involving Medicare fraud. His partner had gotten scared and agreed to cut a deal with the prosecutor and offer proof. Gomez however beat him to the punch. He kidnapped him and, with two hitmen, took him off to the Everglades. Once there, they beat him and found a swampy area with crocodiles and tossed him alive. The authorities were only able to recover a portion of the body, and they owed that to the fact that this wife had immediately contacted them when he didn't return home. By then, Gomez had fled the country. He remained abroad for several years as a fugitive. His accomplices had already been arrested and were serving time while he was living the good life in some corner of the world. His son, whose involvement had never been proven, began sending him money after five years. That was how they managed to find him and extradite him to the United States. He was now awaiting trial. María didn't know what charges had been brought against the son, but she imagined that it had to do with aiding and abetting a fugitive. María wasn't the lead detective in the case but had helped in several aspects.

As soon as she arrived at the office and saw the pastry crumbs on her boss's desk, she knew that Keppler was upset. He always ate Cuban pastries when he was nervous, especially his favorites, the meat-filled pies. His anxiety was also visible in his blue eyes.

"We should have arrested him when we had the chance, *Mariita*." Although she didn't care for it, Duquesne didn't object to the diminutive form of her name. As one of her father's former assistants, Keppler had known her since she was a child and occasionally, in private, still referred to her that way. "We didn't do it since we thought it might be better to stake him out and see where he led us."

"And what happened?"

"An attempt has been made on the lives of the two accomplices in prison. They managed to kill one, and seriously injure the other. I think he and his father are involved."

"So how can I help?"

"Get with Johnson and take a statement from the one who survived, that is, if he makes it. He's already waiting for you at Jackson Hospital."

Keppler and Johnson were the only ones on the force who weren't Cuban-Americans. The boss had studied in Seville, spoke Spanish, and had been married to a Cuban for years. As her father said, he was transplanted Cuban. Johnson on the other hand was another story. Although he had come to Florida at an early age, he had never lost his native Mississippi accent nor, in María's opinion, any of his racial biases, despite hiding them in clever ways. Maybe she was mistaken, but she thought she noticed a subtle gesture of disdain around his lips when he spoke about Hispanics or African-Americans.

Johnson was waiting for her at the door of the injured prisoner's hospital room, where a police officer was standing guard. As soon as they went in, the family members who had been permitted to visit him made their way out.

"*Ay, señorita,* what they did to my son doesn't have a name. Even prisoners aren't safe. How could you all allow this to happen?"

María didn't answer her, but she understood why Keppler had wanted her to come along. Although the prisoner spoke English, the sight of someone from his own culture might help create a sense of confidence and get him to speak more freely.

His statement had to be video-recorded and transcribed by a member of the court, so they had to wait a few more minutes until the entire team had assembled.

It didn't take much prodding to get Gomez to talk. He felt doubly betrayed, and it seemed he didn't care if his account cost him his life. He narrated in extreme detail how they had planned and carried out the 2012 murder, as if it had taken place yesterday. Then he added, as if talking to himself:

"I still have nightmares about seeing that man being eaten by the crocodiles and hearing his screams."

With a faint voice, he told them how he was stabbed in the penitentiary while in line for food and who had done it.

"It was ordered by Gomez... or his son."

Exhausted, he fell asleep.

After she checked in with Keppler who wished her a good weekend, instead of going home and sleeping as she would have preferred, she called her father.

"*Hola Papá*. Are you up for company?"

"What a question. You're not company, and you don't have to call before you stop by."

"Well, I'm heading that way."

"Have you already had lunch?"

"No, but..."

"No, 'buts' about it. It won't take me but a few minutes to whip up a shrimp creole for you that's going to have you licking your fingers."

Since her mother died, more than ten years ago, the father and daughter had become close. As a retired member of the force, he loved to discuss cases with her even though he knew that his daughter couldn't always reveal all the details. The "old man"—as María affectionately called him—had also taken to cooking and the truth was that his dishes were becoming tastier by the day. He no longer followed the recipes verbatim and had started to experiment a bit. Who would have thought it, especially since before he couldn't even make coffee!

As soon as she entered his Westchester house—where years earlier she had lived with her parents—María inhaled deeply the aroma of garlic and spices that was coming from the kitchen.

"Does *that* smell good!" was the first thing she said to her father as he offered her a cold beer.

"As you used to say when you were a baby, the most important thing is… the '*tastess*,'" they both exclaimed in unison and then hugged with a laugh.

Patricio Duquesne's life centered around his daughter and grandson, Patrick, with whom he stayed in close touch. Amazingly, he had learned to send Patrick texts on his iPhone and had even gotten on a bus once to go see Patrick in Gainesville when María was indisposed. Beyond that, he occasionally played dominoes with his friends, he cooked, and—something that horrified María—hunted pythons, an invasive species that was threatening to harm the delicate ecosystem of the Everglades. His daughter thought that maybe he should get out more often and look for a female companion, but each time she suggested something along those lines, her father always replied with the same answer:

"No, María. I was happy with your mother. She was an exceptional woman. No one could ever replace her."

In María's mind, it wasn't a question of loving another woman the way he had his wife of so many years, but rather an issue of having a companion with whom he could grab dinner and a movie.

"Go to the movies? With all the good films there are on Netflix?"

"*Ay Papi.* You know what I mean. To go out dancing, for example."

"But María, I don't dance!"

His daughter always wound up leaving him be. It was true that her mother—María Cristina Fernández Oviedo, who had come from Cuba through Operation Peter Pan before she was eighteen—had always had a certain type of inner strength and quiet affection that not only made her a magnificent nurse but also an unsurpassable wife, mother, and daughter.

María enjoyed her lunch immensely. There was nothing like a home-cooked meal, she thought. Unless her father or companion David cooked for her, she usually got by on salads and yogurt, or occasionally a heavy meal at a restaurant.

Despite the Cuban coffee that her father had made for her, after eating María fell into a deep sleep while sitting in the same recliner where her mother used to nap. Her father had kept it in its exact same spot, and María thought it still smelled like her.

She woke up abruptly and, without knowing why, said:

"A woman could have killed her. Maybe she was limping because she had broken a heel."

She called Fernández and asked him to meet her back at headquarters.

She kissed her father goodbye and almost didn't hear him shout:

"*Mariita*, for God's sake, be careful driving!"

Chapter 10: A Goya?

Day 6, Saturday

When Duquesne arrived back at headquarters, she found Fernández finishing up lunch in the employee's breakroom. He was serving himself a piece of cake.

"Would you like some?" he offered. "It's delicious."

"No, thank you. I just had lunch with my father."

"Well, take a piece with you for later," he insisted while he sliced her a piece and wrapped it up in some foil.

"Was it your birthday?" María asked.

"No, I'm a Virgo. A woman who I really admire invited me to a birthday party for a mutual friend. She throws great parties. There are always writers, painters, professors, pianists… Oh, by the way, she writes detective novels."

María wasn't paying attention to him. She had headed over to the big board that they used to help them visualize the victims and persons of interest in a case. She placed a photo of Sarah Turner's body in the center. On one side, she put her parents, sister, brother-in-law, and Sarah's ex-husband. On the other, she put each one of the Andersons: Eric Sr. and his wife, Elizabeth and her husband, Junior and his wife, and Marty and his partner Yoel. In another section, she wrote the names Aura; Sarah's friend Betty; and a question mark to represent the mysterious man who was seem limping out of the building on the Sunday Sarah was killed. Under each name, she wrote the place where they were at the hour the crime was committed and a number, one to five, to indicate how solid their alibis were.

She took a step back to examine the board.

"What are you thinking?" asked Fernández.

"Well, for the moment, as far as the family goes, I think we only need to dig a bit more into the father and ex-husband. I'm leaning toward the Andersons. The mother has an alibi, but she could have hired someone else, although that doesn't seem to really fit with her style, even if she did know about her husband's affair and the pregnancy. I also don't think it would have been Elizabeth and her husband, and not Marty either. In that family, I'm leaning toward concentrating on the father, Junior, and Yoel."

"For the moment I don't see any reason for her friend Betty to be involved, but I'll look into her like you asked."

"We still need to interview Junior's current wife and his ex. I don't know why it occurred to me that the person who was limping could have been a woman who had broken her heel."

"It could be, but I don't think a woman would have been strong enough to lift her off the floor and place her in the bed like the forensics indicated," Fernández intervened. "Dead bodies weigh a lot."

"That's true. We also don't know what the object was that she was hit with. It had to be metal since there weren't any traces of wooden splinters or pieces of glass in her skull, on the bed, or on the floor. And the murderer probably took the weapon with him."

"We still haven't established if something is missing from the apartment. If that's the case, it's possible that the murderer came to see her, they argued, and in the heat of the moment he picked up some random object and hit her."

"On the other hand, if he brought the object with him, then it was premeditated."

"And we still do not know who fathered the child, but if it was one of the Andersons, anyone in the family could have wanted to see her dead. I don't see anyone else with a motive."

"We have to figure out how we can get the Andersons's DNA," María concluded as she considered the best way to go about obtaining it.

"We haven't compared the list of insured paintings with the ones present in the house. We can't discard the possibility of the theft of a valuable work of art."

"Hmm… do you have the rider from the insurance company? How many paintings were there?"

Fernández looked through the papers in the folder:

"Yes, here they are. There are some twenty or so, and there are photographs of each one."

María looked at her watch. It was after 4:00 in the afternoon. She knew that David was with his sons and that they wouldn't see each other until the next day. She made a quick decision.

"Well, let's get over to Biltmore Way and see if all the paintings are still there."

The insured paintings weren't the same ones that hung on the walls. They were in one of the bedrooms and stored in a special piece of furniture designed solely for that purpose. María and Fernández spent an hour meticulously comparing the canvases with those on the list and the photos provided by the insurance company.

There were various paintings by Cuban artists: Mijares, Calzada, Cundo Bermúdez, Tomas Sánchez, a Mendive, and even a Portocarrero and an Amelia Peláez, all valued for a lot of money, especially the last two. There were other Latin American artists among the collection, such as the Brazilian Guilherme Moraes and the Argentine Marina Font, both residents of Miami and very modern. There were also others that weren't insured, like the ones painted by Sarah's mother. Without a doubt, it was a valuable collection, and the fact that there wasn't a single one missing negated the possibility that the motive had been a robbery.

"Wait, there's an addendum," enthusiastically added Fernández. "There was a painting added later and none other than a Goya!"

Despite searching tirelessly, they couldn't find the canvas, any photograph, and not even a description of the painting or its worth.

María felt that sensation in her stomach that a new clue always produced.

Chapter 11: China

Day 7, Sunday

Over the last three years, María and David's relationship had become more serious. Just like María, he was a detective. He was divorced and had two sons, more or less Patrick's age. Both studied at public universities in Florida. "Davicito," as his Cuban grandmother called him, went to school in Tampa, and Arthur in Tallahassee. David and María had worked together in the past but were stationed in different headquarters some time ago. It was better that way. They spoke and sent texts to each other several times a day and spent almost every weekend together at one of their two houses, usually at hers. They cared for each other, were good friends, and had a lot in common, but she preferred that they live apart. In her opinion, while their kids were single—even though the three of them got along very well—it would be best if both of them had a house that the kids felt like was theirs when they were home on break. David didn't insist, but he would have preferred it if they had gotten married, and he had proposed the idea more than once.

That Sunday morning he arrived early with *café con leche* and Cuban pastries. She was still in bed watching the Sunday morning TV shows that would get her caught up on the week's political events. David brought her breakfast on a tray and climbed into bed beside her. They ate breakfast, watched TV, made love, and then took a long nap. Around 3:00 in the afternoon, they woke up hungry.

"If you want to, we can snack on something light, and then I can take you out to dinner later on," David suggested.

"I don't know, on Sundays all the restaurants are so crowded."

"If I get a reservation at a nice one, we won't have problems. We can go wherever you like."

"*Mi amor*, I'm so tired, and I don't feel like getting dressed. Let's just stay in, and I'll cook."

"No way. You've had a killer week. I'm doing the cooking."

"The problem is there's hardly anything in the refrigerator."

"So, we'll order out for some Chinese food or I'll pick up whatever sounds good to you."

David truly spoiled her, and she was grateful for it.

The two of them wound up eating vegetable lo mein in front of the television.

"Can you believe how soon the kids' spring break is? Does Patrick have plans?"

María had a look of panic on her face.

"Arthur's planning on going all the way to China no less. His girlfriend's sister has been studying there for the semester, and they found a cheap flight. I don't know if David might not get persuaded and go as well, but both of them have promised that they'll come by on Easter Sunday in April. There's still time to plan something if Patrick's coming too."

"I'm not sure what Patrick's going to do. I'll have to give him a call."

"We could do something at my house that Sunday. It'd be great if you invited your mother's friends. I love those crazy old women."

Lourdes and Yolanda had been schoolmates and her mother's best friends. When they diagnosed her with cancer years ago, they had taken charge of everything, from staying with her during the chemo sessions to taking food to her father. When her mother finally lost her battle and passed away, they had adopted her as if she were their own daughter and Patrick their grandson. María didn't know how she would have ever survived without them during those first painful months.

"I appreciate that, but Thanksgivings are always at your house and Easters are at mine. I'll organize it, and I'll let you bring something."

David noticed that she had gotten that sly look on her face that she would get when she remembered something funny, and he couldn't help but ask her what she was thinking about.

"Do you remember when Lourdes was positive that her husband was cheating on her, and what poor Ramon was doing was organizing a hunger strike for the political prisoners in Cuba? She even wanted me to wear a disguise and spy on him!"

Around 11:00 that evening, María began to yawn. David announced that he better head on home. He knew her well and recognized that she needed time to think when she was in the middle of an important case.

Once in bed, María called Patrick. She assumed that she'd get his voicemail and wind up sending him a text, so she was pleasantly surprised when she heard his voice:

"Hi Mom. You won't believe it, but I was just about to give you a call."

"How nice. I've been wrapped up in a case for days, and I don't know what your plans are for your break."

"Well, I have good and bad news."

"Oh really. Tell me."

"The bad news is that I won't be able to be there, but there are two bits of good news."

His flattering tone led her to sense what he was about to say.

"I don't need money, and I promise you we will all be at your house for Easter Sunday."

With the passing of the years, the three young men had become good friends and got along very well. She had an intuition:

"And are you perhaps going to China?"

"Hey, if you were only a detective," he said jokingly.

And he hung up before María could get the chance to tell him to be careful.

Chapter 12: Laura Martin Anderson

Day 8, Monday

María stopped by one of the typical take-out windows where one could drink or grab a Cuban coffee to-go in Miami. She arrived early at the office and was in front of her blank computer screen when Larry Keppler marched into her office and asked her to follow him.

"Have you taken a look at the Pearlstein case, the man accused of raping several young women and sexual trafficking?"

"I didn't think they had assigned it to us."

"You're right. They're handling it downtown, but I guess they're asking us to lend them a hand. They'll have to interview a lot of young women, and they don't have the resources. How much time do you have available?"

"Well, not much really, not until the Sarah Turner case is resolved."

"Do you have a suspect yet?"

"Several, but not one in particular."

"It's usually like that in the beginning. You have to go along eliminating them. What does your gut tell you?"

"It tells me that I still haven't questioned the murderer, and that there's something right there in front of my face that I'm not seeing."

"Well, keep working on it, but keep in mind that I might have to call you in at any moment to spend a day or two helping out on the Pearlstein case. You're good at interviewing minors, and these are delicate matters."

Relieved that she didn't have to drop her case at that very moment, María made two calls. As soon as Fernández came in to the office, she told him:

"Grab the recorder and your note pad, and let's go."

Thirty minutes later, they were at Eric Anderson Jr.'s house in Coral Gables. They hadn't come to see him, rather his wife Laura Martin Anderson

She answered the door dressed very casually, in blue jeans and a Miami Heat t-shirt.

"Shhh…come in, but please be quiet. I just got the baby to sleep."

The detectives knew that Laura had been in a relationship with Junior while he was still married to his first wife, but they had ended their affair. It wasn't until years after his divorce that they met up again. She had graduated with a business administration degree and held a somewhat high position in a banking organization. At the moment, she was on maternity leave.

"How your life changes when you have kids," Laura exclaimed.

María had the feeling that the young woman didn't feel secure yet in her new role as a mother.

"Absolutely. Look, we don't want to take up too much of your time. We just have some routine questions. My partner's going to record the conversation."

"You knew Sarah Turner?"

"Yes. She was always at all of my family's company events."

María detected an annoyed tone in her voice.

Fernández went right to the point:

"Were you jealous of her?"

The young woman flinched and replied dismissively:

"Jealous? No. Why would I be jealous?"

"Well, she was very attractive, and she had a close relationship with your husband. Those types of situations can be difficult for us as women," María replied.

"You're right but, no, I wasn't jealous of her, although I admit I didn't like her very much. She seemed very fake to me, like a knockoff garment or painting."

"What made you think that?"

"I don't know. A woman's instinct. She was a bit of a snob and treated others as if she were superior. And by the way, I didn't meet her through Eric. Sarah had an account at the bank where I work. She was our client. I wasn't in charge of her business matters, but I would see her when she came in, and I waited on her once or twice."

"Sorry, but it's a routine question. Where were you this past Sunday between 6:00 and 8:00 in the evening?"

"Here, with my daughter."

"And your husband?"

"He went to play golf with his father, and he came back around 7:00, maybe 7:15."

"Can someone corroborate that?"

"Perhaps the neighbors saw him come and go, or they could tell you at the Club."

"And you?"

"I don't know. Let's see... I used the computer. I spoke to a friend on the phone. Would that help you?"

"Yes, don't bother. Besides, we don't consider you a suspect," Fernández explained and made a gesture as if he were turning off the tape recorder. It was a way of getting a person to let their guard down.

María took advantage of the moment.

"You haven't been a member of the Anderson's family for very long, and we don't want you to reveal anything personal or secret, but maybe you can help us understand the family dynamic a bit more. Do the brothers get along?"

Laura now seemed more at ease.

"Look, between you and me, Elizabeth and Marty are jealous of Eric. They feel like he's their father's favorite, and it's true but he deserves it because he has a better mind for business, and he works harder."

"And Eric? How does he get along with his father?"

"Very well. He admires him. I think he wants to be like him. Perhaps he competes with his father unnecessarily."

"And Mrs. Anderson?"

"She has a lot of class, and everyone respects her."

"Have you ever met Patricia Duarte, Eric's first wife?"

"Of course. Eric has a son with her, Jack. We occasionally go to Naples to pick him up. Sometimes she brings him here. Come to think of it, I just remembered that on that particular weekend Jack was in Miami, and he called his father to ask if he'd come to one of his games, but I'm not sure what happened because I don't think they met up."

"Did you know her before she married Eric?"

"No. I knew that she existed. I had seen her in photos, but I had never met her."

"And how did she take the divorce, your marriage, and the birth of your daughter?"

"Fine. They got divorced years ago. She hadn't been in love with Eric for quite some time. Without a doubt, my husband is very generous with her and his son financially," she stopped herself as if she realized she had said too much.

"It's probably better if you talk to him about that. These days we all get along really well. It's the best thing for the children. I'm glad I had a girl because I think it would have been difficult for everyone to accept another boy. You know, Jack is the first grandchild, and the only male."

"And how old is he now?"

Laura had to think about it a moment.

"Thirteen, yes, thirteen because last year he became a teenager. He's tall, like Eric."

María thought she detected a certain attitude of tenderness in the woman's voice.

"Well, we've taken up enough of your time."

They got up to leave.

"My pleasure. If there's anything else you need, don't hesitate to call."

Both detectives took her to be sincere.

Chapter 13: Patrick and Jack

Day 9, Tuesday

María wondered if it wouldn't be better to schedule her interview with Patricia Duarte when her son would likely not be home or, on the contrary, at a time when they could question the boy as well. She opted for the first one. Perhaps Eric Anderson's ex-wife would be more forthcoming about her son's father and his family if the young man weren't present. They could always see the boy later on.

The detective thought about that day when she was suffering from a terrible migraine and had asked Keppler if Fernández could go with her to Miami Beach so he could drive. Since then, the two of them had worked as a team. She never dreamed that that skinny, young man would become such a good colleague. He was competent, discreet, kind, and was so knowledgeable about such a wide range of diverse themes that it always surprised Duquesne.

Now Fernández was at the wheel again. They headed down the interstate in silence, each one engrossed in their own thoughts, which actually were not that far apart since both of them were going over everything they had learned during the case. Finally, María asked her partner:

"So? What do you make of it?"

"I don't know. You go first. You have more experience, and that intuition of yours rarely fails you."

"Things don't add up. We've been basing everything on the theory that one of the Andersons was the father of Sarah's baby and that the motive for the crime was to eliminate another possible heir to the fortune, but there are a lot of unanswered questions. Not only do we not know who the father is, we're not certain who knew about the pregnancy. And besides, I don't think that family could resort to murder. The danger of being caught would be greater than merely sharing a piece of the inheritance."

"Yeah, but it could have been an accident, an argument that went awry."

"Maybe, but I think there's something we're not seeing, and it's right in front of our faces."

"I haven't had time yet to find out too much about her friend Betty or her ex-husband. And we should also keep exploring the matter of the paintings. That business about a painting by Goya just can't be true. It must be some crazy Cuban who decided to take his name as a moniker. He probably paints cans of black beans for the Goya brand."

"You're right. We have to look into the painting, but I thought it would be best to try to rule out members of the Anderson family first."

Before they headed to Patricia Duarte's house, they stopped to get a bite to eat at a local bistro on 5th Avenue in downtown Naples. The weather was beautiful, so they decided to eat at a table outside. María ordered a salad with various types of greens and nuts, dried tomatoes, goat cheese, sweet onions, and wild mushrooms, all doused in a balsamic dressing. It was delicious, and she was pleased that she hadn't gone off her diet. Thanks to her spinning classes and changes in eating habits, she had managed to lose fifteen pounds two years ago, and she had maintained a steady weight since then.

Fernández ordered some quesadillas covered in a green sauce with avocado, Manchego cheese, and pico de gallo. It looked good. María was happy that she didn't find out until after he had finished that they were made with crocodile meat because just thinking about it made her gag.

"Oh María, you're very refined. Since I was a kid, I've always eaten just about everything."

Both of them finished with an espresso. Although it was nothing like the coffee they were used to in Miami, it wasn't bad.

They finally headed off for Patricia Duarte's house, some twenty-five minutes from downtown. It wasn't necessarily a luxurious mansion, but it was inarguably a rather large house for a mother and son in a nice neighborhood. On the way there, Fernández informed her that the house was in Patricia's name, what it had cost her, year of purchase, and what she paid in taxes."

"Oh yeah, and it's paid off."

"Her 'ex' must have bought it for her," María sighed, perhaps due to how little Bill helped her, including with Patrick's expenses.

"Maybe, but don't count on it. She's nobody's fool. She graduated from Harvard with a degree in Computer Science, and she has a good job at NewsBank."

María was surprised at how tall Patricia was. She didn't know why she had formed a different image of her, one which vanished immediately as soon as she saw her. She also realized right away that she was an intelligent and polite woman.

After the customary introductory remarks, and having turned on the tape recorder, María began with her questions:

"Tell me how you met Eric Anderson, Jr., what was your courtship like, your marriage, your divorce."

Patricia—as people often do during questioning—sighed deeply before answering.

"Well, I was born in Miami. My father is from El Salvador and my mother from Costa Rica. Both from very good families. I was educated in private Catholic schools. I played basketball and was also good in science, a rare combination for a Latina. I didn't think I would have a chance of getting in, but the counselors encouraged me to apply to Harvard. Even when they accepted me, I didn't think I could go because of the cost. My parents don't lack for money, but they aren't rich either. Harvard however has a sliding scale for tuition based on your parents' income, and they even gave me a basketball scholarship. In short, I happily took off for Cambridge, ready to take on the world. During my first year, I didn't have time for anything other than my studies and athletics, but I was happy. In my second year, I met Eric. He was handsome and kind. I had hardly dated any guys at all, and I don't know if I fell in love with him, or if I found it flattering that he paid attention to me. The thing is I lost my virginity to him. I don't regret it, but it wasn't how I had imagined my first amorous experience would be. Eric, on the other hand, knew—or I guess, knows—how to seduce women. There were months when he couldn't go two days without seeing me, without being with me, you know... without having sex. To be honest with you, I didn't put up a fight. I grew to like him more each day. But as my mother always said, '*if the pitcher goes to the well once too often....*' Despite our precautions, I wound up pregnant. I thought that it was the end of the world because I still needed two more years to graduate from Harvard, and I didn't want to withdraw from school."

Patricia interrupted her story. As she had done when they arrived, she once again offered the detectives something to drink, and before they could answer she had already taken off for the kitchen and returned with three bottles of cold water. She drank half of hers before she continued to speak:

"Well, I must tell you I was surprised by Eric's reaction. He immediately told me that he would pay for an abortion, and not to worry that it was legal and safe. In spite of my desire to continue my studies, my Catholic upbringing wouldn't allow me to consider that option. And I don't regret it either. My son is my greatest treasure. Well, to make a long story short, although he was a bit reluctant, Eric married me. We had a simple wedding. Just a Justice of the Peace and a couple of friends were present. Even though I asked him several times, he always refused to have a church wedding. Since he wasn't Catholic, I didn't insist. We moved into a dorm for married couples. I was lucky that Jack (we named him after my father, Joaquin Duarte) was born in May, so I didn't miss a single semester of classes, only that summer which I spent primarily in Miami with my parents. When I returned to Harvard in August with the baby, things with Eric went from bad to worse. He seldom helped me with the baby, and he soon went back to his old ways of being the carefree student, as if he weren't married and didn't have a child. I realize now that we were both very young. In short, we mutually decided to get a divorce a year later. He graduated and went off to Pennsylvania to continue his studies at Wharton. I stayed to finish mine. Obviously, I had to stop playing basketball, but I had good grades so they didn't take away my scholarship. Aside from that, Eric regularly sent me a check on the first of each month. Regardless, it wasn't easy to continue my studies with a young one. Occasionally my mother would come spend a few days with me during exams. In short, I graduated when Jack was two years old, and I went back to Miami."

"And during that time, you didn't meet Eric's family?"

"You won't believe it, but he hid our marriage and his son's birth from his family. They finally found out, and they read him the riot act. They met the child. They all take care of him. What I mean is, I'm not hurting economically speaking. His father sees him quite often, and has taken trips with him, including one time he took him to London on a business trip. The grandparents and Eric's siblings are relatively affectionate. They send him birthday and Christmas gifts. They've included us in a few family reunions but there's always, I don't know, a notable distance, an invisible line that separates us, maybe because I'm Hispanic or from a different social and economic class. It doesn't really bother me, but I feel bad for my son."

"How long have you lived here in Naples? Why did you decide to move here?"

"Almost five years now. As I told you, I graduated from Harvard with a degree in Computer Science. When I got to Miami, I was exhausted and didn't start working until Jack started school. The truth of the matter is that we were able to live well on what Eric sent us, even though it wasn't extravagant. Finally, I accepted a position in the library at the University of Miami, and I began making my own way. One day someone told me about the opportunity at NewsBank, and I applied. I'm always surprised when these types of things work out, but after two interviews they offered me the job. As you know, NewsBank has its headquarters here in Naples, although I work from home for a considerable part of the time these days. Miami has become a pain with so much traffic— pardon me for saying so since you both live there. My parents were about to retire, and the idea of doing so in Naples appealed to them. It's so lovely and calm here, even though it's a bit expensive. I thought it would also be good for Jack, and so that's what we did. His father doesn't complain about paying for his private tuition. Jack started at St. John Neumann High School this year, and he plays football for the Celtics. My parents and I didn't know a thing about that sport, but we've learned and we don't miss a game."

"And how does Jack get along with Eric and the rest of the Andersons?"

"Very well. I believe he was a little jealous when his little sister was born. I'm glad they had a girl because that way he's still the only grandson. My impression is that his grandparents pay more attention to him for that reason. They want him to spend next summer with them, but we'll see."

"You don't really care for the Andersons?"

"It's not that. They're my son's family, and I will always try to make sure that he has a good relationship with his father and the rest. Now that the years have gone by, I realize that my relationship with Eric was a mistake. As I told you before, I don't regret it. They're people of high class and wealth, but obviously they have different values than those of my family, which is not to say that I have something against them."

María saw Patricia look at her watch.

"It's just that I have to go pick up Jack at school," she explained.

"I understand. Only a couple more questions. Your son was in Miami last weekend, wasn't he?"

"Yes. His school had a football game there, which is unusual. He rode with his friend Bill and his parents because I had to finish up some important work for Monday. He came back on the school bus with his friends, a bit perturbed because his father had forgotten about the game and didn't come. He didn't fill me in on the details. I don't know if you have kids, but teenage boys are intolerable. Sometimes he only replies with a grunt, if he answers at all. And yet, he's always been a good and serious boy."

"I completely understand. I have a twenty-four-year-old son, and he went through the same stage."

Patricia looked at her watch again, and stood up.

Fernández, who had remained silent, intervened:

106

"Could we talk to Jack?"

The woman seemed annoyed.

"I would prefer not to involve him in this."

"I realize that, but since he was in Miami we have to establish his whereabouts at the time the crime was committed."

Patricia lost her composure that she had kept throughout the interview.

"Look. He is a child. How could you possibly think he could kill someone?"

"No," María clarified, "we don't think that. But our job requires us to rule out everyone, and the sooner we do, the sooner we can leave you and Jack alone."

As Patricia thought about it, Fernández, with a softer tone in his voice this time, suggested:

"Look, we will be glad to do this however you prefer. If you want to, we can accompany you to the school and meet him there. Or, we can wait outside in the car until you come back with him. We'll ask two quick questions when you return, and we'll be on our way. That way we don't have to come back again."

Patricia agreed begrudgingly, but as they headed out to wait in the car, she told them:

"Stay here inside. Policemen aren't going to steal anything."

María insisted that they wait outside.

It didn't take her more than a half hour before she came back with her son.

"The game was on Sunday afternoon and ended around 6:00. We won. Coach took us all out for pizza afterwards. I didn't pay attention to where exactly the place was. We went on the bus, and I'm not as familiar with Miami as I used to be. Bill's parents came back to Naples when the game was over, and I came back on the bus with the team. Mami picked me up at the school around 9:30, I think."

The detectives assured them that was all and then offered a friendly goodbye.

When they turned the corner, María asked Fernández:

"Did you notice?"

"Yes. Jack was limping. We'll have to look into why."

Chapter 14: The White Head

Day 10, Wednesday

The sound of her cell phone woke her up at 7:00 in the morning. She had programmed it to have different ringtones for the various individuals in her most intimate circle. When she heard the John Philip Sousa march, *El Capitan*, she knew her boss was on the line. Larry Keppler almost never called with good news.

"Did I wake you up, Mariita? I know you've been hard at work on the Biltmore Way case. How's it coming?"

"Well, okay. We have a few leads, but nothing really concrete, to tell you the truth."

María waited. She knew that Keppler hadn't called just to get caught up on her pending case.

"Look, I'm sorry to interrupt your work, but I had mentioned to you earlier that I might need you to interview some minors implicated in the case regarding the millionaire Pearlstein. Can you be here by 9:00 this morning?"

"Sure. What's up?"

"It has to do with one of the young girls who's accusing him, but the DA hasn't been able to get all the details. He thinks that if a woman interviews her she might be able to get the girl to open up. You're very good at that sort of thing."

"How old is she?"

"Fourteen." She perceived a hint of sadness in the voice of her boss, who had a granddaughter more or less the same age.

Two hours later, seated in one of the interrogation rooms, a young girl with long, dark hair was in front of María. Since she was resting her head on the table over her folded arms, at first María could only make out the crown of her head.

"Hi Ludmila. I'm María."

The young girl lifted her head and showed her face for just a second, but it was long enough for the detective to see in her eyes the traces of pain and shame that she shouldn't have had to experience at such a young age.

"Would you like a cold drink, a coffee, some water?"

She did not answer. María placed a cold Coca-Cola in front of her that she had brought with her.

"Look Ludmila. You haven't done anything wrong. I'm here to make sure that the people who have hurt you receive their punishment. I want to help you."

The girl barely moved.

María placed her chair alongside the girl's and gently put her hand on her shoulder.

"Ludmila, you have nothing to be ashamed of. What happened wasn't your fault. I know that you're suffering, but you're going to feel better once you tell me everything and once you confront your abuser."

The young girl suddenly recoiled.

"Not that. I don't want to see him ever again. Never. Do you understand?"

"Well, you don't have to decide that right now. I only need you to tell me what happened."

Little by little, the girl kept moving in her chair until she was face to face with María.

"I don't know where to begin."

"To start with, let's see, where are you from?"

"My mother was born in Ukraine, and my father is Cuban. They met when he was studying in Odessa. After *perestroika,* he refused to go back to Cuba. They came to Miami in the early 1990s when my brother was young. More than ten years later, I was born. They say I was a 'change of life baby.'"

For the first time María saw a trace of a smile on the young girl's face.

"They named me Ludmila after my Russian grandmother, even though I never met her or my Cuban grandmother either."

María didn't want to pressure her by asking direct questions.

"And where do you go to school?"

"I started High School this year, but this all happened when I was in Jr. High, two years ago."

"You were twelve years old then?"

"Yes. Almost thirteen."

"How did it all start?"

"You won't believe it. There was this teacher that we all really liked. She was like a friend. Well, she wasn't really a teacher. She was the trainer for the girls' soccer team that I was on. Sometimes she'd take the whole team out to eat at McDonald's. Then there was this other time when she invited us to her house. When we got there, there were a lot of other adults who said hello to us and shook our hand before they took off. It just seemed like they were treating us as if we were somebody important, and I liked it."

The girl stopped her story, and María waited a few seconds.

"What happened next, Ludmila?"

"A few days later, she invited us to her house for a snack. Not everybody, just two or three of us. She told us we were old enough to start being independent, and we deserved it, but our parents still hadn't realized that we were young women and they were treating us like little girls, even though they meant well. She added that in order to be independent the first thing we had to do was pay our own way, and that way we could buy things and go places without having to ask someone else for money. That seemed make sense to all of us, and we got excited. She started out by giving us small chores around her house: trimming a few plants in her garden, helping her arrange a closet, the same things that they would always ask me to do at home but I would play dumb so I didn't have to do them. But Miss Versen paid us, and we liked having our own cash."

Ludmila opened her Coke and took a big swallow.

"Would you like a glass with some ice?"

"No, don't bother. It's still cold."

"And then what happened?"

"One day I was alone at her house. I didn't know that my other friends weren't coming. She told me that she had a special job for me and that I could earn enough money to get that cell phone that she knew I had been dying to buy, but that we had to leave that second and she would take me. I wanted to call my mother and ask her but she talked me out of it. She reminded me that I was old enough to make my own decisions, and if I turned her down she'd have to let one of the other girls have the chance. Regardless of how much I asked her what it involved, she never gave me a straight answer, only that it was easy."

"Where did she take you? Do you know the address? The area?"

"I don't know. She took the interstate north for a half hour or more. Then she took off on one of the exits. She turned two or three times and then parked in the back of a building. There were some stairs. She told me to go up and then they'd instruct me what I had to do once I got up there. I asked if she was going to wait for me. She explained that she wasn't, but that once I was done they'd take me back home in a car. That seemed strange to me, but by then I was already standing in the parking lot, and Miss Versen was taking off in her car. I didn't have any other choice but to go on up. I'll never forget those stairs that were so narrow and dark. Finally, someone opened a door, and there was a large bedroom with a bathroom, a brown shag rug, and a sofa that was about the same color, just a bit lighter. I don't know why I remember those details. Everything was dark, and the air conditioner was going full blast. When my eyes finally adjusted, I saw a dresser with a mirror and a massage table. There was a clock on the wall."

Ludmila paused again, and María waited.

"Almost right away a man with white hair, who was only covered up with a towel, came in. He came in talking on the phone in a language that I didn't recognize. It wasn't Russian, or English, or Spanish, and I don't think it was, French, Italian, or Portuguese either. Maybe it was German. I don't know. He laid face down on the bed, and he told me to massage his back, his legs and his feet. I tried to do it the best I could, even though he was overweight and my hands aren't real strong."

Just then, Ludmila lowered her head and spoke so softly that María had to make a concerted effort to understand her.

"The second he got off the phone, he turned over and lay there completely naked. I had never seen a thing so big on a man. I had only seen my brother peeing once before when I accidentally walked in on him in the bathroom. My mouth dropped open. When he told me to get undressed, I was scared but I did it. I stood there with only my underwear on. I was shaking because I was so scared and cold."

The young girl began to bawl. María let her sob and waited until she could resume.

"What happened next?"

Then Ludmila looked directly at her.

"Can you believe he set the alarm on his phone? Then he sat up and took off my bra. With one hand, he masturbated and with the other, he fingered me. He told me to pinch his breasts. I had a hard time finding them because I just wanted to keep my eyes fixed on the clock so I wouldn't remember a single thing about what was going on, but in reality all I could see was his big white head, the white head of that monster that was telling me to pinch his breasts harder. It lasted for fifteen minutes. Finally, there was like a loud groan, and a thick and milky liquid came out of him. He smiled at me and told me that I could go then, and that there was a car waiting for me downstairs that would take me home."

Ludmila started to cry again with deep silent sobs as if the monster's white head was still preventing her from voicing her pain. María got up and put her arms around the girl's shoulders until she could calm down.

As soon as the young girl left with her mother, the detective ran to the bathroom and threw up her breakfast and Coke.

Chapter 15: Vizcaya

Day 10, Wednesday

María was still in the ladies room when she heard a knock on the door, followed by Fernández's voice.

"Hurry up, María. Hurry up. There's been another murder."

As soon as she came out, her assistant informed her that a woman's body had been found in the gardens at Vizcaya Palace.

"Let's go. Keppler said for us to head over there ASAP."

On the way, they wondered if there could be any connection between the two crimes. The one involving Sarah's murder had taken place in her apartment in a high-rise condominium in Coral Gables but this one was in a very public place. The only thing they knew was that the victim was a young, attractive female, which for the moment was the only similarity they could find with the Biltmore Way case.

María asked Fernández if he had ever visited the Vizcaya Museum and Gardens.

"Yeah, I've been several times, especially for poetry readings and Renaissance festivals, but they stopped doing those years ago. I think it was because they were just too successful... and the place would get too packed. How about you?"

"I went years ago with my school and once to a wedding. It was like something out of a fairy tale..."

María wanted to brush up on the history of the place, so on the way over she got on the Internet and read how more than a century ago James Deering, a US business tycoon, had instructed three men to design and construct a European-style palace and gardens to be used as his winter retreat. Although they did not complete it until 1922, and Deering died three years later, he was still able to spend many enjoyable days there. From Christmas Day in 1916 until his death, he spent several months there every year, usually from mid-November to mid-April. He threw lavish parties, and once he even brought in gondolas from Venice. As one might expect, among those invited, there were many famous guests. In 1952, Dade County acquired the property and converted it into a museum, which subsequently made the registry as a National Historic Landmark. In addition to its French and Italian designs, Vizcaya was famous for its open-air fountains and statues.

"They've been refurbishing and restoring it for the centennial anniversary coming up in 2022, even though they had already commemorated it in 2016," Fernández—who always seemed to know every-thing—informed her. "These anniversaries are always good to bring in funding. They charge for everything around here, but it has to be expensive to maintain it."

By the time they arrived, the forensic team had already cordoned off the area as a crime scene. Everyone was busy taking photos and collecting evidence. María was surprised to see Dr. John Erwin there. He usually sent his assistant to do the fieldwork since he preferred the task of unraveling the clues that lay hidden within cadavers. In fact, he always said that not only can the dead speak, but they're always the best witnesses to their own murders.

Dr. Erwin immediately called them over. María couldn't help but be shocked when she saw the young woman, dressed completely in black, lying in the garden with one arm extended and her hand resting in the bay water. Fernández jumped back as if he had seen a ghost.

Erwin kept on speaking, but it took them a few seconds to compose themselves and to pay attention. The doctor showed them the victim's head. It looked like she had received a blow to the head similar to that of Sarah Turner with the only difference being that there wasn't any blood mixed in her hair, which this time was brunette with highlighted streaks.

"I don't know if you realized it," Fernández said as if coming out of a trance. "She looks identical to the way Lillian Gish appeared in that movie they made… *Way Down East…*"

He was referring to a famous scene in which the renowned actress of silent movies gets lost in a snow storm. They were able to create the scene with so such realism that the director himself was afraid the actress was going to freeze to death. The film debuted in 1920 and Gish often visited Deering's house in those years.

"Well, there's obviously no snow around here," Erwin said in an attempt to relieve the tension since the more facts they uncovered the more it seemed to all of them that the crime scene was increasingly becoming more bizarre.

"I can't be sure of anything until I examine her in the morgue, but to me it looks like they didn't kill her here and that she didn't die from the head wound. And it looks like she's been dead for several days."

Duquesne had already given the orders not to allow anyone to leave from Vizcaya. With the new information in hand, she called in more help, took a picture of each tourist and their driver's licenses, requested a phone number from each of them where they could be reached, and then sent them on their way. She was hoping she was not mistaken, but none of them had seemed suspicious.

Next came the process of interrogating the employees who worked there. María focused on the ones that worked in the gardens and that had been present the night before. She soon found out that for the price of admission, each attendee had received a gin cocktail and that they all danced to a jazz orchestra dressed in costumes from the 1920s. Typical of the era, the victim wore a black, flapper dress, a thin headband around her forehead, and a long strand of pearls. However, she was bundled up in an overcoat, something completely out of sync with Miami's climate. A pair of black gloves and a long cigarette holder, with a half-smoked cigarette, had been carefully placed at her side.

For the first time in her career, María felt confused. She didn't know how to make sense of it all. Had the victim been one of the attendees at the party the night before and the resemblance between her and the scene with the famous actress merely a coincidence? Did it have something to do with the death of Sarah Turner? Were they looking for a serial killer?

One of museum curators came up and whispered to her, "We haven't had time to do a complete inventory, but I just realized that there's something missing."

"Go ahead."

"I don´t know if you're aware that we sponsor art programs. We have a workshop. We were getting an exhibit ready and one of the paintings is missing."

"Is it valuable? Who's the painter?"

"It's someone very young, so even though he's in high demand, the painting isn't as valuable as many other things that we have… I wouldn't know what it's worth… I'd have to check on it."

"And what's his name? What nationality is he?

"He's Spanish. Gregorio Ibarra, but he signs his paintings as GoyA."

Chapter 16: Unanswered Questions

Day 11, Thursday

For María, spinning on her stationary bike, the constant going up and down, and sweating through every pore of her body, not only gave her energy but it also helped her think. Sometimes it was almost an unconscious process, but one thing for sure was that when she finished up, she always seemed to see things more clearly.

After she had her coffee and finished her exercise that morning, she decided that while she waited for Dr. Erwin to identify the victim and provide her with more information, she would focus on the Biltmore Way case.

Fernández, who knew Duquesne well, already had some important new details for her when she got to the office.

"So, I spoke with Jack's coach. He told me that the young man had twisted his ankle at the beginning of the game, and he had to pull him. He presumes that he was there the whole time with his teammates, but he can't swear to it. The game lasted two hours and forty-five minutes, and it took place at Coral Gables High School."

"Even though it's in the general vicinity, the boy couldn't have walked all the way from there to Sarah's apartment and especially with a sprained ankle."

"No, but he could have taken an Uber, a taxi, a bus, or even hopped on the Coral Gables trolley for part of the way. He had enough time to get there and back."

"But Fernández, he's just a child. Do you really think that…?"

"I personally don't have an opinion. I'm just giving you the facts that you asked for. Right now I was about to go see what I could find out about Sarah's ex, her friend Betty, and also Yoel."

"Fine, and get the names, addresses, and phone numbers of Jack's closest friends on the team. As soon as we can, we'll go see them. If we still have any doubts, we'll have to look into what type of transportation he could have used and if there are any security cameras that got a glimpse of him. Meanwhile, I'll try to find out more about this painter who signs his name as 'GoyA.'"

"I already found out something, which I was just about to tell you. His name is Gregorio Alberto Ibarra.

As you know, sometimes people with the name Gregorio go by the name Goyo. So, he started signing his name that way, and then later on he placed the "o" inside of the "A" of Alberto, and his squiggle ended up looking like the signature of the famous Spanish painter. He takes his inspiration from him, and even inserts figures from Goya's paintings into his own works, but he's a modern artist. Others have used that technique before, like Emilio Falero who used to insert some of Velazquez's figures into his works."

María spent some time on the Web and confirmed that everything that her colleague had said was true as well as some other facts. She learned that in the art world forgeries were commonplace. The modern ones were easy for the experts to spot; however, in the case of Goya, one of his contemporaries—Eugenio Lucas Velazquez, who bore no relationship to his fellow seventeenth-century compatriot, Diego—had forged more than seven-hundred Goyas. As a young artist he apparently practiced by copying the Master's works in the Prado Museum. Later on, Lucas—who was a young man when Goya died—became very successful with his own works. Maybe he wasn't the one who had sold the copies that he had made when he was young.

"María, can you stop by and see me today?" It was the voice of the forensic examiner on her cell. She didn't ask him anything. If he wanted her to stop by, there must be something that he didn't want to discuss on the phone.

The schools were closed that week so there was less traffic than usual. It didn't take her anytime to arrive at the red-brick building that she had visited so many times before, home of the Forensic Pathology Department for Miami-Dade County. Before she got out of the car, she grabbed the sweater that she usually kept in the back seat. It was always frighteningly cold in there.

She knew she had to be patient with Dr. Erwin. He was a perfectionist with his work, and he didn't like to share information until he had proof. Besides, he tended to give curt explanations unless the case sparked some type of enthusiasm in him, meaning, when the answers didn't come easily.

As soon as she went in, María knew that the good doctor would only provide her with parts of the puzzle that she herself would have to piece together.

"So, here you have the fingerprints. And here, are some other details including her weight, height, and a photo of her face in case you need it later for identification purposes."

María took the papers and waited for more.

"The first thing I can tell you is that she'd been dead for five days and kept in a refrigerator or at least a very cold place. Secondly, someone had sex with her after she was dead. And third, her stomach is completely destroyed. The cause of death was not the blow to her head. That was made *postmortem*. And it wasn't with the same instrument that killed Sarah Turner, although it was similar."

"What killed her then?"

"They cut her stomach open to remove something."

"Drugs?"

"That's the most likely thing, but I can't count out anything. It could have been diamonds, for example…. One more thing. Whoever did it, tried to close her back up. The stomach was stitched up carefully. There are even parts that look like they've been embroidered."

"Wow, a creative murderer."

"Indeed."

"Then you don't think that there's any connection with the murder of Sarah Turner?"

"I can't determine that. From a forensic point of view, they are very different crimes."

"How do you know that there was sex involved? Was there semen? Some bit of DNA we could use?"

"There is something we'll be able to process. I'll let you know once I have it."

María stayed for a moment longer and thought things over. Dr. Erwin was already working on another autopsy. She walked through the halls and back to her car like a robot. She was leaving with more questions than she had when got there.

Chapter 17: An Old Friend

Day 12, Friday

The calendar on her watch reminded her that it was Joaquin del Roble's birthday. María smiled. Her friend was getting old and weak, but mentally he could still think very clearly. She had met him some four years earlier when they had re-opened the case of a missing child that disappeared a few days after Hurricane Andrew had devastated the region. Don Joaquin—the uncle of the young man who had drowned when his car went into one of the canals— had been a great help to her, and ever since then she would call to check on him and even go by and visit him in The Palace, a retirement home for senior citizens where he lived.

When they first met, del Roble had told her his life story. During the Spanish Civil War, his father was taken prisoner and ultimately executed. He and his mother and brother went through hard times until an uncle, who had immigrated to Cuba, helped them leave and go to Havana. Once there, their mother made a living by making hats for high-society women. Joaquin and his brother delivered them and

129

took care of the money. The majority of the responsibility fell upon Joaquin, even though he was younger, because his brother was deaf and mute. Even decades later, Don Joaquin still clearly remembered the streets and avenues of the Cuban capital that he had crisscrossed so many times in his youth. Despite her brother's opposition, the boys' mother decided to try her luck in New York, where things went very well for her. She fell in love and married a man of means who paid for her sons' education. Joaquin graduated with a degree in electrical engineering, but he never went into the profession. Instead, he dedicated himself to doing technical translations. He and his wife, Antonia, never had any children, and when she, his brother, and his parents passed away, he moved to Miami so he could escape the cold, which he detested. He started up an alarm company, and he made his way along until old age led him to retire and move from his small house in West Gables to The Palace. If María's calculations were correct, he was turning ninety-four or ninety-five.

Even though she had to go out of her way and was in the middle of two cases, she decided that before heading to the office, she would go by and wish Don Joaquin well. She got out a bottle of Chivas Regal that she had recently received, wrapped it up well, and hid it in her purse. Every evening her friend liked to drink two fingers of Scotch, or *güisqui* as he called it. These days the nurses allowed him to do it because they had realized that it agreed with him. Every once in a while, there would be a rookie employee who hid it from him, but the head nurse would always retrieve his "medicine," as he referred to his favorite alcoholic libation.

"I know it's not the best time, but I wanted to come by to congratulate you and bring you a gift," María said as she greeted him.

"You're the only one who keeps track of this old fool, and even my birthday!"

"So how many years is it, old friend?"

"I don't know. I've lost count. Ninety and some change."

"Well, give me a heads up before you reach one-hundred so we can throw a huge party..."

Don Joaquin made a gesture with his hand as if he were swatting away flies.

"Oh, *mijita*, I've already lived long enough."

"Don't say that."

"No one needs me anymore."

"Well I do. Look, right this very moment I'm tangled up in a case and you can probably help me."

María didn't tell him any details about the two murders specifically, only that the first involved an inventory of some valuable paintings and an addendum that included a Goya. She also explained about Gregorio Alberto Ibarra, alias GoyA, and the other painting that had disappeared.

"You must know something about the Spanish painter that could help me."

As if he were travelling back in time, Don Joaquin hesitated for a few seconds before answering.

"Well, regarding that Gregorio fellow I've never heard anything about him, but as for the real Goya I know a few things. I've already told you that we're from Villanueva de Jiloca, a small town in the Zaragoza province. You can't imagine what a small village it was. I mean, *is* not *was*, because there's only a handful of people living there these days according to what I learned from a letter from the grandchild of a friend of mine who passed away. The community is tucked away up in the hills. In my childhood, I loved those pine trees, poplars, vineyards, gardens, and fruit orchards… and the Jiloca river. Oh, the times we had when all of us boys would go for a swim in its waters. And how we enjoyed the festivals in honor of the Virgin of Rosario and St. Gregory. They were in August. Sometimes we'd combine our festivities with those from another nearby town, Nombrevilla. Can you believe it? I can't always remember the name of the nurse who brings me my meals every single day, but I can still see the village crystal clear: the church, the immense bell tower where the storks made their nests, the wooden portico, the *mudéjar* style archway, and my father who was always complaining about the parish priest. Back then, I thought he was right, but I'm not so sure these days."

María waited patiently because she sensed that her friend would get around to telling her about Francisco de Goya, but he needed to wade through all these memories first.

"Anyway, it's like all of that belonged to someone else's life. Since my younger brother died, I no longer have anyone that I can talk to about these types of things. I apologize for so much preamble just to tell you that I only went to the provincial capital, Zaragoza, on two occasions. The first time was when I was a child. My mother took my brother and me because one of her cousins lived there, and she needed to discuss a family matter with her. Her cousin's husband took us around the town, along with his daughter who was a bit older than us, while the women stayed behind and gossiped. I'll never forget what an impression the immense *Basílica de la Virgen del Pilar* made on me. Oh, now I remember. That was the name of the girl, and they called her little

Pilar—"*Pilarica.*" I'm sure she must have passed away by now. I always remembered her as a skinny little know-it-all that never stopped talking and somehow seemed surprised when my brother and I didn't know what she was talking about. Inside the basilica he showed us a fresco by Goya, and her father proudly told us that he was the most important Spanish artist and, naturally, he was from Zaragoza."

Don Joaquin unexpectedly asked María:

"Did you know that your Jose Marti lived there and studied at the University of Zaragoza?"

"Yes, I did. I've read about it, and my parents told me about it too. I even remember a few of his verses: "For Aragon in Spain / in my heart I hold / Aragon the whole / frank, fierce, faithful and sane.""

Don Joaquin smiled.

"A man who dedicated his life to fight against Spain but could still write something like that, he must have been great."

"When was the next time you went back to Zaragoza?"

"I don't want to even think about the second time. It was during the war. I saw horrific things."

"And Goya?"

"The truth is the only thing I knew about Goya as a kid is what I just recounted. Maybe I had seen some copies of his work somewhere. I also don't remember learning too much about him while in Cuba. Later on, when I went to study in New York, some friends encouraged me to take an Art History class. They said it was easy, and besides the teacher was good-looking. I had the misfortune that at the last moment, they changed professors, and I got stuck with an old, ugly guy, but he was a Spanish exile and had a real passion for Goya. That's where I learned a lot about the artist. And I think that same year there was an exhibit of some of Goya's paintings at New York University, and the professor took us to see it. Years later, in the 1960s, I saw another exhibit in New York. I remember I went with my wife Antonia and my mother. I even bought each one of them a book about his artwork. Antonia liked his courtly paintings, but I liked the ones depicting the beggars and the one about the executions, even though it reminded me of my father and made me sad."

"It's my understanding that there are still some Goya paintings in New York, right?"

"Yes, more than anything else, there are some etchings at the Met. A few years ago, there was a big scandal because they discovered that some of them were fake. However, the most important Goya, at least at that time, was at The Hispanic Society. It's a portrait of the Duchess of Alba, but not like the more famous ones in which she's lying down, clothed in one and nude in the other. In this one, she's standing, dressed in black. I remember it because for a while I worked near that building, on Broadway and 155th, and I would go every once in a while with a fellow Spaniard and colleague from work to see the paintings. The ones by Sorolla really made us feel nostalgic. You know very well that the greatest ill of all exiles is nostalgia, or that special melancholy homesickness that the Galicians call *morriña*."

"And you've never returned to Spain?"

"Yes, I decided to go back some fifteen years ago, right when I was about to turn eighty. Before Franco died, I never thought about going back. Then, almost one after another, my relatives began to die, and I figured it didn't make sense to go back. But in the end, I went back."

"And what did you feel?"

"That's a long story. I felt, I don't know, like I was born again, and at the same time I was dead to everything. You're very young. You couldn't understand."

María took out the bottle of Chivas Regal and placed it on the table.

"It's a bit early to have a drink, but I promise you…"

At that very moment, her cell rang and she gave a quick goodbye.

"I'm sorry. It's the station, and I have to get there right away. I don't know when, but I promise you I'll come back soon so we can share that drink. One of these afternoons."

Although Don Joaquin usually kissed her hand in a chivalric gesture that moved her, this time without thinking about it María leaned down and kissed the old Spanish exile on the forehead. She noticed that her friend's eyes had teared up.

Chapter 18: The Limousine

Day 12, Friday

María was heading back to the station, consumed with the analysis of so many loose ends, when her phone rang. It was Patrick. He was calling from the Montreal airport on his way to Shanghai with Davicito, Arturo, and his girlfriend Amy.

"*Mami*, I just got through eating a Cuban sandwich. Do you know how lucky I am to find a Cuban sandwich in a Canadian airport!"

"And was it any good?"

"Yeah, you bet it was. The bread was a little different than what you get at Versailles or La Carreta, but it was really good."

"*Hijo*, take really good care of yourself. Do you have a jacket with you? I think it's been chilly over there."

"Yes, *Mami*, don't worry."

"And stick together. Don't get lost. There's over twenty-four million people in that city!"

"I see that you've been doing your homework on the internet. *Mami*, how am I going to get lost considering how tall I am? They could find me right away in any crowd, no matter how many Chinese there were."

Patrick let out a laugh in the same way that María's father always did, and she couldn't keep herself from doing the same.

When she got to the office, Fernández approached her:

"Come on and I'll get you caught up before we meet with Keppler. They've identified the body in the Vizcaya homicide."

"Is that what the press is calling it?"

"No, I think the Museum has tried to keep a lid on it, and for the moment it hasn't been linked to the one on Biltmore Way, but Keppler is worried because now we have two unsolved murders."

"Me too. So, what have you found out?"

"The victim arrived a week ago from Mexico with a Peruvian passport under the name Isabel Flores, but it was a forgery. She's from Nicaragua. Apparently, there's a network of drug traffickers that use women who are desperate to come to the US. They provide them with false papers. The women swallow the drugs in balloons, they expel them—as you can imagine how—then they give them some money to start a new life, and they remain in the US as undocumented immigrants. If they're caught in the airport, as is sometimes the case, they're on their own. But the biggest problem for the drug 'mules' is that sometimes the balloons burst inside of them and they don't notice."

"It doesn't surprise me. Is that what happened to her?"

"Yes, but it looks like there were other complications. Another thing, she had family here, and…"

They saw that Keppler was motioning to them to come into his office. María thought that her boss looked like death warmed over. He seemed nervous. He sighed deeply and made a noticeable effort to speak calmly:

"Guys, we have to solve these two crimes. I don't know what you think, but I believe there's a connection between the two of them. As for the one at Vizcaya, we need to focus only on whoever's responsible for killing the woman. The DEA will take charge of the contraband network. That's out of our jurisdiction. On another note, Sarah Turner's sister called. She wants to know if there's been any developments and when can she come collect the things in the apartment. She'd like to do it tomorrow, but I told her to give us a few more days. Please, I need you to work both cases 24/7 if that's what it takes."

"Don't worry. We're on it."

María and Fernández retreated to the conference room to work out a strategy.

"I think the first thing we have to do is interview the son of the Nicaraguan woman."

It didn't take them long to find him, and the young man showed up at the station one hour later.

"I had told her not to do it. I had told her a thousand times."

"Okay, so, tell us everything from the beginning."

"I don't know where to begin. So… my grandmother came here years ago. I hadn't even been born yet. She, umm… well, I guess I should just tell you everything. Despite all the years that she's been here, she still doesn't have her documents. She comes from a poor family. She didn't know how to read or write, but she's a hard worker. She left my mother and her two brothers with an aunt, and with the help of an agency, she managed to get them to pay her way and get here under a contract, supposedly as a housekeeper, but they practically kept her here as a slave. She managed to get out of it with the help of the Jehovah's Witnesses. I don't believe in all of that, but the truth is they helped her a lot, and she even learned to read and write in order to study the Bible."

"And your mother?"

"My mother! As a kid, I remember my father, who was a drunk, always hitting her until one day he took off and never came back again. *Mami* picked herself up and, with what my grandmother sent us, she would buy things and then re-sell them. I always teased her and told her that she had the soul of a hustler, or a *bisnera* as the Cubans say. She was really stubborn. When she got something in her head, she didn't stop until she had her way. Since my grandmother couldn't go back, my mother decided that we'd find a way to come visit her. I don't know how she was able to arrange it—it's been such a long time ago—but she managed to get a student visa for me, and a multiple-entry one for her. I completed my studies. I married a girl who was a citizen, and now I am too. We have a two-year-old son. We love each other a lot, so don't think that I got married just so I could get my green card."

"And your mother?"

"*Mami* would come every three or four months. She'd clean houses with my grandmother, and buy things to sell back home. She had an old, little car she used when she was here, and she bought a pretty nice van back there. She was getting ahead. I was surprised at how much she changed physically. She lost some weight, put some highlights in her hair, got her nails done, dressed nicely, and behaved and spoke differently compared to my grandmother. In short, she became more upscale. She was so happy when my son was born! Even though she was such a tease and never wanted to be called grandma..." for the first time the young man's voice cracked and he had to make an effort not to break down and cry.

María reached over and handed him a glass of water.

"I'm sorry... It's just that it still seems like a nightmare to me."

"What was your mother's name?"

"Esmeralda Reyes. My grandmother named her Esmeralda after a character on a soap opera. And I'm Roberto Jardines."

"Had she transported drugs before?"

"No, it was the first time. What happened was that they didn't renew her visa. It had almost been a year since she was allowed in. She was dying to see my grandmother, me and my wife, and above all her grandson. Besides, the money she earned here is what allowed her to be better off there. My grandmother and I sent her what we could, but in Miami everything is so expensive. Half of what you earn goes just to pay the rent. And obviously, it's worse there. I don't know if you've kept up with it, but things have gone from bad to worse in Nicaragua. And my mother's life wasn't like it was when she used to earn just a few bucks here. Besides, she had gotten used to the good life."

"Were you aware that she was transporting drugs?"

"Yes and no. I didn't know for sure, but I suspected something. The last few times we spoke, she told me not to worry, that we were going to see each other sooner than I could imagine. It was impossible that they were going to give her a visa, so I feared that she was involved in something that wasn't legit. I told her not to even think about coming over the Mexican border—you know, with all the problems they have there—and she assured me that she wouldn't."

"And why did you assume she might be bringing drugs? Do you know someone in the cartel?"

"No, I assure you I don't."

"So, what happened next?"

"Last Sunday I got a call from her asking me to come pick her up, and she gave me an address that was a little strange, sort of near the back of the airport.

She told me to hurry because she didn't feel well. I took off right away to go get her. It took me longer than it should have because despite the GPS I got lost. I finally found her in an alleyway, lying next to a dumpster. Just as I got close, another car came up. Two guys got out. They shoved her in, and they sped off with my mother inside the car. My first instinct was to call the police, but then it occurred to me that my mom was probably tangled up in something bad, and I'd better not do it. Now I regret it, because I followed the car, I tried to call her on her cell, but nothing. I was so worried. I still haven't told my grandmother anything. I had the feeling that something bad was going to happen. And then you guys called me, and today I went to the morgue to identify her body."

"Do you remember what the car looked like?"

"It was a long, black car, like the ones they use at weddings. I'm not sure what model, but I believe it was a Cadillac. Oh yeah, I got the plate number before they got on the interstate and I lost them. Here's the photo."

As if he couldn't take it anymore, the young man broke down and cried. María and Fernández left him so he could grieve in private.

Chapter 19: Fingerprints

Day 12, Friday

María unexpectedly realized that the accumulated tension and fatigue was overtaking her entire body even though her mind was still racing non-stop. She asked Fernández to look into the license plate that Esmeralda Reyes' son had taken down and to find out who it belonged to, and then she told him that she'd be gone for a few hours. She headed over to her father's house unannounced. Even in the unlikely event he wasn't home, she had a key. What she needed most was to spend some downtime resting in her mother's old armchair. Over the years, the pain caused by her absence had become less acute, and it had turned into a tender and safe place in her heart. She could talk about her with her father, her son, and with her mother's friends without her voice cracking, and she could even look at old photographs without breaking down in tears. Even after all this time, if a recipe or note in her mom's handwriting fell out of a cookbook or turned up in a drawer, seeing her mother's calligraphy with its parallel, round, and harmonious Palmer penmanship would bring about an emotional jolt.

Her father gave her a hug when she came in. He knew her well enough not to bombard her with questions right away. Instead, he only said:

"Are you hungry? I've already eaten lunch, but I can fix you something."

"What do you have?"

"I don't know," said her father opening the refrigerator. "I can offer you anything from a beer and some delicious cheese that I bought yesterday to a bowl of chicken soup that my neighbor Luisa brought over. It's really tasty, and you know there's always ham, turkey…"

For María the chicken soup was a godsend. She thought it was just a Cuban thing, but over the years, she had come to learn that it was a "cure all" in many societies, including Jewish and American cultures as well. It not only cured the body's maladies, but it was good for the soul too. Her father served her the soup with some Cuban crackers. It was the only place where she ate them, and they too brought her a type of spiritual peace and sense of security. There, in that house, in that Westchester neighborhood where she had grown up, next to that old policeman and wonderful father that Patricio Duquesne was, she would always be safe and sound.

She finished her lunch and fell sound asleep. An hour later, her cell phone woke her up. When she went to answer it, she realized that her father had been watching her sleep, just as she would do sometimes with her own son Patrick. She knew how much love there is in that almost always anonymous act of keeping vigil over a loved one's sleep.

Fernández told her that the evidence from the forensic team regarding the fingerprints in Sarah Turner's apartment had arrived, and that there were a few clues about the vehicle that had kidnapped the Nicaraguan woman.

"I'm on my way."

She arrived in less than twenty minutes.

"What do you have?"

"So, some of the fingerprints are the ones that we expected to find. Naturally, both Andersons, the son and the father, Betty her friend and neighbor, Aura who cleans for her, and Sarah herself, of course. There are two sets that we haven't been able to identify. They found one pair in the bedroom where she kept the paintings, and they belong to a man who apparently doesn't have a criminal record. The other ones, given their size, probably belong to a child or

148

teenager, also without a criminal record. They found these on the doorknob of the front door and also on the arm of an armchair in the living room."

"Do you think they could belong to Jack?"

"That was my first hunch."

"Let's interview his friends first before asking his mother to bring him in so we can get his fingerprints. And what about the wedding limo that they used to kidnap the woman?"

"It wasn't a wedding limo. It looks like it belonged to a funeral home in Hollywood."

"No way!"

"What should we do first?"

María looked at her watch.

"Let's interview Jack's friends."

"Do you want to drive all the way back to Naples again?"

"No, I found out that they have another game here in Miami this afternoon."

They were in luck. Jack wasn't there because, according to the coach, his sprained ankle was still swollen, and the doctor had ordered rest and ice for three more days. When minors are only witnesses and not suspects, it is not mandatory for police to interview them in the presence of their mother or father, but the majority of the parents were at the game and they explained to them what it was all about. María suspected that young people were less forthcoming in the presence of adults, but there wasn't always another option.

All the players on the team said the same: that Jack had taken off from the game rather quickly, and that they didn't remember if he had been with the team the entire time. They all agreed that he had eaten pizza with them and returned to Naples together on the bus. María was convinced that they were hiding something to protect their friend, but there weren't any contradictions or doubts in the way the young men told their account. It dawned on her that they hadn't interviewed Bill, Jack's best friend. They weren't able to do so until the game was over since he was one of the stars on the team. Although he said the same thing as the rest of them, in the middle of his story María realized that he wasn't telling the truth. There was a certain way he avoided making eye contact that gave him away. She tried to frighten him:

"Bill, lying to a police officer is a crime. If Jack wasn't with you the entire time that doesn't necessarily mean anything bad. Maybe he went to see his father or grandfather. He has family here. We're going to find out, so it's better if you tell us the truth."

The detective saw that the young man was on the verge of telling them something, but right then his mother came in and insisted that they leave.

"We're back to square one," Fernández replied.

"Yes and no. On the one hand, we know that there's a clue to follow here because there's something fishy going on. On other hand, I don't know… it's hard for me to believe that the young man went there to kill Sarah. Why would he do that?"

"Maybe he overheard a conversation that he wasn't supposed to hear, or he saw a text, or in some way he found out that she had gotten pregnant by his father or his grandfather, and he was jealous…."

"My intuition tells me that he's lying, but that he's not guilty."

"What do you want to do about the funeral home in Hollywood? There are two viewings tonight and a burial service tomorrow at 11:00 in the morning and another at 3:00 in the afternoon."

"I'm dead tired. I'll see you at the office at 9:00 in the morning and we'll go to the funeral home before the 11:00 burial. Sound okay?"

María spent the night with David but she didn't sleep well. She didn't fall asleep until it was almost morning, and she received a text from Patrick saying that he had arrived safely in Shanghai. Besides knowing that her son was on such a long flight, she worried about the two unsolved cases that still didn't offer any clear leads.

David knew her well and they didn't speak a lot. He could tell when she needed her mental space to think. In the morning, he fixed her a nice breakfast.

"I'm sure you haven't eaten much these days."

"That's true. Except for some chicken soup that my father fixed for me today, just junk food. Thank you... and not only for breakfast," she said and then gave him a hug.

She left as soon as she took her last sip of coffee. She didn't think it was appropriate to bother God with these types of things, but she couldn't help saying a personal prayer:

"Please, God, guide my way in solving these two cases."

Chapter 20: The Bodies

Day 13, Saturday

Considering it was a Saturday morning, there was a lot of movement inside the police station. María was concentrating so much on her own affairs that she wasn't sure what her colleagues were working on. *I'll get up to speed on things once my two cases are solved*, she thought.

Fernández was waiting for her. He knew she preferred to use her time in the car to think about things.

"If you want me to, I can drive," he offered. "I think it'd be best if I went by way of North Palmetto and then take the Turnpike. Sound okay?"

"Whatever you think. Regardless, it's going to take us at least an hour, don't you think? It's 9:00 now, so we're okay on time. I wonder if it would've been better to have made an appointment with the Funeral Director."

"No, I think we're doing the right thing showing up without tipping them off."

"You're like my father: *'Forewarned is forearmed'*. Right?"

"Right. The element of surprise in any interrogation or investigation always gives you an advantage. People don't have time to invent alibis or hide evidence."

"I sure hope you're right."

María liked Hollywood, a small city in Broward County between Miami and Ft. Lauderdale, with its quaint parks and above all several miles of beaches and a broad boardwalk that had an abundance of hotels and restaurants, all of which were more economical and less crowded than the ones in Miami Beach. The area had grown considerably since the beginning of the 1970s when many Caucasians moved north fleeing the avalanche of Hispanics that had arrived in Miami. There was even a joke that people would tell, "The last American to leave, don't forget to take the flag." Obviously, there were also Hispanics in Hollywood now, but not like in Miami.

It didn't take them an hour to get there as María had predicted. After forty-five minutes they took the Turnpike exit and two minutes later they were on Taft Avenue in front of a a red-brick house with white columns, an ample parking lot, a carefully landscaped yard, and a sign that read Joseph Baker Funeral

154

Home. There weren't too many cars there at that early hour of the morning. As soon as they went in, a middle-aged man with hair and a mustache that matched his gray suit said:

"Can I help you?"

"We'd like to see the Director."

"If you've experienced, or fear, a painful familial event and you need our services, I can be of assistance."

"No, it's not that. We need to see him regarding another matter. Is he in?"

"Yes, just a moment, please. I'll let him know," and he showed them to a waiting room.

María was surprised by how bright the sun generously shone through the windows. She had almost always been to funerals in the evening, and hadn't imagined how things would look in the morning.

A few minutes later, Mr. Ted Light came in, dressed in a suit that was identical to the previous gentleman's, and with the same plastic smile. He showed them in to an office that was comfortable but not ostentatious.

"How can I help you?"

María identified herself and also introduced Fernández. Both of them showed the man their badges. The detective waited a few minutes before speaking. She thought she noticed a slight twinge in the right eyelid of Mr. Light. Was he possibly nervous?

The first thing that she did was to take out her laptop and pull up the photo of the limousine that Esmeralda Reyes' son had taken, and asked him bluntly:

"This limousine belongs to you, correct?"

"Yes. Is there a problem?"

"We're not sure. We've come to find out. Is the vehicle here at this moment?"

"I'm not sure."

"Can we take a look?"

"There's no need for you to bother. I can call down and they can tell me right away. Even better, all I have to do is look on the computer."

He looked at the screen next to him, and then back to them:

"It just so happens that it's out for a burial service at 11:00."

"Is it taking the family members of the deceased?"

"Yes."

"And do you have another limousine that's available?"

"Obviously, but tell me, what's the problem?"

"We need to take it with us."

"Do you have a warrant?"

"No, but we can return with one, and not only one for the vehicle but to search the entire premises. Even better, Fernández call headquarters and tell them to send one over. We can wait here until it arrives, unless you cooperate."

"Obviously I will, but I don't know what this is all about."

"Is your name really Mr. Light?" Fernández abruptly asked him in Spanish.

The man responded in Spanish as well.

"No, young man. My name is Teodoro Luz. My paternal grandfather used to say that we were descendants of Jose de la Luz y Caballero. You know who that it is, right?"

"Of course. The great nineteenth-century professor and Cuban intellectual," Fernández immediately replied.

"Yes, an illustrious last name, but for Americans it's easier just to go by Ted Light. I always tell them that I hope I can be a 'light' for them in these difficult moments. You know, you have to do what it takes to earn a living."

To an extent, the tension had lifted.

"Look, Teodoro, this car was seen this past Tuesday in Miami. It was used to kidnap a woman and later she was found dead."

"But that can't be! Virgen de la Caridad del Cobre!"

Deep inside, María was amused and thought: *these Cubans, always invoking a saint or a virgin.*

Teodoro began to tell them how he had left Cuba on a raft in 1994 and had remained at the base in Guantánamo for a year before gaining entrance to the United States. María interrupted him in order to get back to her questions. She knew that if you let a Cuban keep going, they'd recount their entire life at the drop of a hat. In the end, however, the man was of great assistance. He instructed them to bring the limousine in question back to the funeral home, and he sent a different one for the family members of the deceased. While they waited for the vehicle to arrive and the forensic team that would take it from there, Teodoro didn't stop talking:

"I'm glad that you're here. To tell you the truth, for a while I've been thinking that some strange things might be going on here."

"What type of strange things?"

"Well, like sometimes they cremate a corpse and all the ashes don't fit in the urn. That's strange, don't you think? The person in charge just smiles and says that the person was overweight, but I know that's not how it works. And can you believe it, they wind up dumping out some of the ashes. Imagine if they family found out. I try to downplay it with a friendly tone, but it's true and it would be a scandal. I also irritate him by asking 'Perhaps you stuck more than one in there?' And he smiles like he's nervous."

"And what else have you observed?"

"I don't know if it's all in my head, but it seems like the caskets weigh too much."

"Why would that be?"

"You probably think my imagination is working overtime. It's almost always when some elderly, thin person dies who doesn't weigh a lot. I've wondered if maybe they haven't placed another corpse in the same casket."

"And why would they do that?"

"The only thing I can think of is that maybe someone who doesn't have a burial plot might be paying them to bury them like that."

"Do you suspect anyone?"

"The truth is there's a strange guy who started working here about a year ago. I've been here ten. He often stays here alone at night. We close at 12:00 or no later than 12:30. It's not like in Cuba where there's a wake all night long. But he doesn't always leave with the rest of us who can't wait to get out of here. He looks for excuses to stay behind and says he'll close up. I don't why they gave him the keys with so little time here."

"Is the individual here now? What's his name?"

"No, today is his day off. His name is Peter Raymond. He's an American and that's his real name, or at least as far as I know."

"And what's his job here?"

"Mainly he gets the bodies ready. You know, he dresses them with the clothes the family brings in, he does the hair, puts on makeup. Sometimes he needs help, but usually he does it by himself. He says he likes his job. I personally don't like that part at all. I only have to deal with the families, not the corpses."

"Can you show us where he works?"

"I believe so. He doesn't like us to go in there, but the owner has never said we couldn't, and when it comes to the police I have an obligation to cooperate. Come on, come this way."

María entered the basement room a bit hesitantly, but Fernández immediately began to inspect everything as if he were an expert in the field. After a few moments, he said:

"María, come over here. Look at this. The casket has a false bottom. Without a doubt there's enough room underneath to fit another corpse."

Chapter 21: The Calm

Day 14, Sunday

María was still going to her spinning classes at least three times a week, but that Sunday she decided to sleep in. As always, she woke up early, and was glad to feel David's body next to her. A few seconds later, he got up but insisted that she keep sleeping. She did so until almost 10:00 in the morning.

Later on, drinking their coffee in their respective recliners, the couple watched their customary Sunday TV programs on political news and commentary that would get them caught up on what had been happening in the country that week.

María couldn't concentrate. She looked again at the two photographs that Patrick had sent her from Shanghai. Her son had always been formal, but he had matured even more so in recent years. He was a man now. She remembered how happy and proud she had felt last May when they all went to his graduation at the University of Florida. And by "all" she wasn't kidding. His grandfather wouldn't have missed it for anything. He couldn't have been more puffed up with pride! Her ex-husband, Bill, went with a companion who turned out to be quite nice. Then there was David, along with his two sons, and Patrick's godmothers—her mother's friends, Lourdes and Yolanda who went loaded down with gifts. Several of his friends graduated that same day, including Mathilda, the young Haitian girl who had suffered so much during the earthquake that took her grandmother and parents. Mathilda's aunt and uncle from New York who had taken her in were also there.

That evening they all went out to eat at a restaurant where they had made a reservation, without which it would have been impossible to dine out. Gainesville was full of families that were celebrating the culmination of their son's and daughter's education. When it came time to pay the bill, her father grabbed the check, an act that was immediately followed by David taking out his credit card. To her surprise, Bill, who had always been somewhat stingy, did the same. And when Mathilda's uncle offered his card too, Patrick looked disapprovingly at the three men and said:

"Let us treat. Mathilda has helped me so much over the years and my family would like to show you our gratitude."

María saw how his grandfather beamed with complicity. They didn't let Lourdes or Yolanda pay either. They were being so typically Hispanic, and maybe even chauvinistic, but it seemed charming to María.

Patrick had decided to stay in Gainesville and pursue a Masters, a decision that everyone supported, especially since he had received a scholarship. He had worked for three years for the football team's digital department. He was one of the members who filmed and edited the Gators' videos. That's how he had often been able to get tickets to the games, and how they had come to be participants in the enthusiasm of the "Swamp" on several occasions. They had met some of the players who were Patrick's friends. That stage of her son's life that he had enjoyed so much was about to come to a close since he would finish his Masters in August. He had already said that he didn't want to participate again in the graduation ceremony. María would have like him to do so, but ever since he was a child she always tried to respect his wishes and let him make his own decisions whenever it was possible. She preferred to deny him permission only in matters of the utmost importance, and the young man knew that if she said no, it was impossible to convince her to the contrary. What concerned her was what Patrick would do now that his studies were ending in a few months. She was anxious to talk to him about it once he got back next weekend.

She was so fixated on looking at the graduation photos on her phone and thinking about things that David had to repeat his question twice:

"Want me to make you some breakfast?"

"Oh yeah. Yes. Would you like some help?"

"No thanks. Just tell me what you'd like, as if you were at Denny's."

"Your breakfasts are much better. Surprise me. Everything you make is delicious."

A few minutes later, David placed a tray on the table in front of her with orange juice, a spinach and feta omelet, a toasted croissant, and two small blueberry muffins.

"Would you like more coffee?"

"I'll get it."

"Nothing of the sort. Hand me your cup. Today is a day for you to rest and be spoiled. You've had a hell of a week."

It was true that David spoiled her, and she wasn't sure if she showed him enough appreciation. In order to compete in a man's world, especially in a career like hers, she had learned to keep her emotions under control, and she feared that it sometimes caused her to appear indifferent to those she loved the most. And David, without a doubt, was a great companion. With that in mind, she turned to him with a broad smile and said:

"You're so good to me, David. I love you."

He returned her smile and put her at ease.

"I know. And I love you too."

Even though she hadn't gotten up until almost 10:00, María leaned back in the recliner and fell asleep again with the Sunday paper in her lap.

Around 4:00 in the afternoon, her father called to invite them over to have some chicken and rice. María didn't really feel like getting dressed and hesitated. Patricio seemed to read her mind:

"Come as you are. Put on some jeans and T-shirt, and put your hair up in a ponytail. You always look beautiful no matter what."

She gave in, and it turned out that Lourdes and her husband were there too, along with Luisa, her father's neighbor. Patricio had gotten the domino table ready and while he and Luisa finished cooking and setting the table, Lourdes, Roberto, David and María sat down to play. The four of them played very well, and the scores were close and the laughs plenty.

Lourdes and Roberto lost so they got up in order to let Patricio and Luisa have their turn while the rice was simmering.

"One of the things that I like about dominoes," Patricio declared, "is that the loser gets up and gives the others a chance. It's the only thing that Cubans do like that, because when it comes to politics...."

They had a great time together, and María was glad she had decided to accept her father's invitation. They were already heading back to the house when her phone rang. She was surprised that Eric Anderson would call her on a Sunday night at 10:00. She immediately noticed that what had appeared to be a sense of calm when he spoke was really masking his restlessness.

"I need to see you right away."

"Right now? Is something wrong?"

"No... well, yes, but I have to see you in person."

"Do you want to meet me down at the station?"

"Yes. That's the perfect place. But look, it'd be better if we met tomorrow morning, at 9:00 sharp."

"I'll be expecting you."

"I'll be there with my lawyer."

"If you think it's necessary..."

"Duquesne, I'm going to turn myself in. I killed Sarah Turner."

Chapter 22: The Confession

Day 15, Monday

María wasn't listening to the girl who served her Cuban coffee at the walkup window at the café where she usually stopped on her way to work. She was too focused on last night's call from Anderson. If he had really killed Sarah, how hadn't they figured it out? The cameras showed him at her apartment on Saturday, not Sunday. She was so distracted that she almost left without paying.

"Don't worry ma'am. I wasn't going to call the police," the girl said jokingly.

Fernández, whom she had informed about Anderson's call the previous night, was already at the station when she arrived at 8:30 in the morning. Together they got the interrogation room ready, with its two-way mirror that would let them observe from the outside without being seen, and the camera they'd use to record the interview.

Anderson arrived at 9:00 sharp, well-dressed and respectable, but with a face that showed that he hadn't slept at all the night before. He was accompanied by Joseph L. Weiner, a well-known criminal defense attorney. He had a broad forehead and was almost bald, but he also had long, curly gray hair that started halfway back on his scalp, like a mane. His white beard and mustache framed his perfect teeth. He was famous for winning cases, even before they came to trial, frequently based on the defense that the prosecutors had obtained evidence illegally. It bothered María terribly that criminals went unpunished merely based on what she considered to be tricks by their defense attorneys. Even though Anderson had declared that he was coming in to surrender to the authorities, the fact that he had hired Weiner as a lawyer made her feel uneasy.

They were still greeting each other and making introductions when Susan Lanuza Brown came in, another lawyer from Weiner's firm. *He has come well protected*, María thought to herself.

They finally got settled in in the interrogation room: Anderson and his lawyers sat on one side of the table, María and Fernández on the other. She had asked Keppler to observe through the two-way mirror. It was an important case, and she didn't want there to be any slip-ups.

"What can you tell us, Mr. Anderson?"

"We'd like the record to show that Mr. Anderson has come voluntarily on his accord," Weiner interjected.

"Yes, of course."

Anderson blurted out:

"I killed her. I'm sorry. You can arrest me."

Weiner looked at him like a father does a small child. Before María could reply, he advised his client:

"Eric, you need to explain what took place, and how things happened."

Anderson began to speak as if he were reciting a memorized text.

"I told you that I was there on Saturday and, when I left, Sarah was fine. That's true. But I didn't tell you what we argued about. The previous week she had told that me she was pregnant and that she was going to get an abortion. Actually, she didn't tell me that the baby was mine, but I figured it was. I told her to think about it, that I wasn't going to get a divorce, but that I would help her financially if she wanted to keep the baby. She told me she'd think about it."

Anderson paused and took a drink of water from the bottle they had placed in front of him.

"That Saturday she told me she had changed her mind. She was going to have the baby, she wanted a million dollars, and I had to acknowledge that the child was mine. I told her that I would, but later on I started asking myself if the child was really even mine or not because we had ended our relationship a month and a half ago. I went back on Sunday. We argued. I flew off the handle, I shook her, she fell to the floor, and hit her head. It was an accident. But I should have called 911, and not left her there."

María was convinced that Anderson was lying. Who was he trying to protect? She knew it would be easy to prove that his version of the facts were inaccurate.

"Where did you leave her?"

"In her apartment."

"Yes, but where exactly?"

"I told you. She fell."

"Where did she fall, Mr. Anderson?"

"Mr. Anderson was in shock. It's normal that he can't remember all the details," the female lawyer intervened.

"Did you take her pulse? Are you sure she was dead?"

Anderson paused.

"She didn't move. She didn't answer."

"But you leaned over her? You checked to make sure she wasn't breathing."

"No, but..."

"What time did this all occur?"

"I don't know, maybe a little after 6:00 or 7:00, after I left the club but before I went home. Everything happened so fast."

"And through what means did you enter and exit the building without appearing on the security cameras?"

"Through the back."

"Why? Did you go with the idea of killing her?"

"Of course not! I just wanted to be discreet."

"And you have a key to the building's parking garage?"

"No, but when a couple came in, I took advantage of it and followed them in."

"So, they would remember having seen you, because on the tapes we can identify who came in through that door."

"I don't know. Maybe not. I was behind them. Maybe they didn't see me."

María knew that Anderson wasn't telling the truth. Among other things, they had found Sarah on the bed and not on the floor, a fact that they hadn't shared with the press and not even with the family. She told them to wait and she went out to consult with Keppler.

"I think if we arrest him, he'll dig himself into a deeper hole with his lies and we'll be able to figure out who he's protecting," she said to Keppler.

"Yes, but if the murderer isn't a member of the family, I wouldn't want to arrest him for no reason."

"Chief, he's handing himself in. We didn't go after him."

"Well, I'll trust your intuition."

María went back in the interrogation room, read Anderson his rights, and informed him he was under arrest. She asked Fernández to take him to the main office to be booked.

"We'll pay the bail right away," the lawyer said.

Anderson looked at her with immense sadness. He uttered softly:

"I would prefer if there weren't much press, for my family's sake."

"That's not up to us," she answered with her Duquesne frankness, but down deep she felt sorry for that business magnate who was sacrificing himself for someone in his family. Was it his son? His grandson?

"Fernández, do a DNA test. We have to find out if he's the father of the child that Sarah Turner was expecting."

Weiner immediately objected.

"We will file a motion to exclude that information."

"And you'll get your chance to discuss that with the prosecutor and the judge," María answered as she looked him right in the eyes.

Did the lawyer know his client was innocent? Did he know who the true guilty party was?

They all got up. Fernández got out his handcuffs.

"Is that necessary?" Weiner asked.

María doubted that it was, but even if she believed he was innocent, Mr. Anderson didn't deserve special treatment because of his social and economic position.

"Yes, it's standard procedure," and she nodded to Fernández to go ahead.

She imagined what lay in store for Eric Anderson over the next few hours, and she thought about how much he must really love the person he was protecting. But she couldn't allow her personal feelings to get in the way of her professional conduct. The best thing she could do right now for Anderson and for Sarah Turner was to find the real guilty party.

Chapter 23: Up On The Table

Day 15, Monday

Just as Fernández was escorting Anderson out in handcuffs, with his lawyers behind him, María's cell phone rang. It was Bill, her ex-husband. By the tone of his voice, she could tell he had come in peace, which she appreciated because she wasn't in the mood for anything else—or as her grandmother used to say, "the oven isn't ready for those cookies." He had received the same photo from Patrick in Shanghai as she had but with the not so subtle and disturbing text: "The Chinese Uncle Sam is always watching everybody all the time."

"I don't know how it could have dawned on him to write such a thing."

"Yes, it was a mistake, but I don't think there'll be any consequences," she said trying to calm him down.

"When does he get back?"

"I think on Friday, and they'll spend the weekend in Miami. I'm dying to see him."

"Me too. María, has Patrick talked to you about his plans after he finishes his Masters?"

"No. And you?"

"No. And each time I bring it up, he avoids my questions."

"I think he's just not sure what he wants to do."

María saw Keppler gesturing her over. She told Bill she had to hang up, and headed to her boss's office.

I just got a call from the Broward County Police. I think you had better head over there. I'll tell Fernández to meet you once he's done.

"What's happened?"

"I'm not sure. I know they've arrested a couple of employees from the funeral home, and they want us to collaborate with them since the Esmeralda Reyes case is still pending and our forensic department still has the limousine."

Although she had to pay attention to the traffic, which was getting worse in Miami every day, María took advantage of the drive over to think about things. She had two murders to solve, one of a white, educated, affluent woman who lived in a building in a fabulous neighborhood where she should have been safe. She probably knew her killer because there weren't any signs of forced entry into the apartment, and she was placed on the bed and even covered up. For the moment, there only appeared to be one missing painting, signed by "GoyA," which she didn't believe to be worth too much on the market compared to those by other artists that weren't taken. Sarah Turner was expecting a baby, and since the very beginning she had suspected that the father was some member of the Anderson family, given that if it belonged to the father or the son, a lot of money was involved. Now that the father had turned himself in, she had ruled him out because his version of events didn't line up with the facts. That very confession led her to believe that he was protecting someone in the family; however, even though she had interviewed each member of the family, her intuition had eliminated all of them. Who, then, had the motive to kill Sarah Turner?

Esmeralda Reyes, on the other hand, was a woman of limited means, a Nicaraguan who entered the country with false documentation after her visa to the United States had not been renewed and who had transported drugs in balloons that she swallowed. One had exploded inside of her, and they cut open her stomach to remove the rest of the drugs. She had shown up at the Vizcaya Palace, dressed in a costume from the 1920s, found lying in a position that Fernández said resembled a scene from a silent film.

To make things worse, Dr. Erwin reported that the cadaver had been kept on ice for several days and that it had been sexually violated post-mortem. She had heard about cases like this, but she had never investigated one. Nevertheless, she immediately thought about the funeral worker that Teodoro Luz had described who was a little odd and who remained at work at night alone with the deceased.

The only connection between the two murders was the work of art by the Spanish painter who had a fellowship in Vizcaya and, for the moment, neither the artist nor the painting could be found. She was still a few minutes away from the Hollywood police station when her cell phone rang. She had requested information about Gregorio Alberto Ibarra and asked that they try to find him. The station informed her that he had flown to Spain two weeks ago and that he was scheduled to return that afternoon. They sent his flight information, his photo, telephone number, and Miami address to her tablet. He didn't have a criminal record, at least not in the United States.

The number of people in the police station surprised María. Some were obviously federal agents. She recognized them immediately. *Something big must be going on*, she thought to herself.

It seemed like they were waiting for her. The Chief of Police himself, Chris O'Donnell—a man about her own age, who was as proud of his Irish roots as she was of her Cuban ones, and whom she had seen on a number of other occasions—took her to his office right away to get her up to speed.

"So, the Feds are working on a lead about a large drug operation. They've arrested two men at the Joseph Baker Funeral Home on Taft Avenue. They're also suspicious about some other irregularities at the funeral home. We're supposed to work on those, but they want us to keep it away from the press. They figure they have bigger fish to fry with the drug trafficking than the minor things at the funeral home, and they don't want the big cats to get wind of it and take off. I know you've been over there and, granted, you could have given me a heads up, but I'm not going to make a big deal of it now that we need to work together. In addition to one of the funeral home limousines being implicated in the murder that you're investigating, maybe it was also involved in trans- porting drugs too. The Feds don't want any infor- mation leaking about the matter, and they want us to leave it to them. Still, we're supposed to interrogate the two suspects. I'll let you take lead chair since the murder is the primary issue for the moment."

"Thanks. What are their names?"

"Peter Raymond and Ted Light. Which one do you want to see first?"

"The light that leads is the one that shines." Since she uttered that particular phrase in Spanish, O'Donnell didn't understand her play on words.

"First, Ted Light," she explained.

As soon as she entered the interrogation room, Teodoro Luz' face lit up. He couldn't stop talking.

"*Ay, señorita*, please! Tell them I didn't have anything to do with this."

"Sit down Teodoro," she told him in English in a severe tone. "I don't think that you were being completely honest with me the other day and that you've seen a lot more things."

Teodoro remained quiet.

"You know that the first one who talks gets the better deal. If you cooperate, I can see to it that you don't come out badly in this mess you've gotten yourself in to, but you have to tell me everything and tell me now."

The man continued to be silent.

"As an accomplice to murder, you're looking at spending a lot of years behind bars."

The detective stood up and headed toward the door.

"Wait, wait. I'll tell you everything, but I don't want to go to prison. Promise me…"

"I can't promise you anything until you tell us something first. The only thing I can say is that they will treat you as fairly as possible."

"Look, I didn't do anything wrong. They only gave me money, and I looked the other way. That's all, and I nearly told you the other day because I was starting to get nervous. There were a lot of things."

"So, Teodoro, did they hide drugs at the funeral home?"

"Yes, but I don't know what type or any other details. I think they bring them in at the crack of dawn, and Peter keeps an eye on them. They take them out little by little as they sell them."

"And where does Peter keep them?"

"In plain sight, in one of the coffins. It's one of the cheapest ones and no one would buy it. It's in the basement."

"Do you know the names or any detail about the people who brought in or took out the drugs?"

"No. Well, one time without meaning to—because believe me, the less I know the better—I caught a glimpse of one of them, but fortunately he didn't realize it."

"What did he look like?"

"What can I tell you? Normal. I just saw him for a few seconds."

"And what else is going on at the funeral home, Teodoro? What's going on with the bodies?"

"Look, I don't know how many times it's happened. I've only seen it twice. They've brought in dead women to Peter and he buries them, he cremates them, he makes them disappear."

María thought it was an implausible way of getting rid of a cadaver.

"When was that?"

"The first instance was a long time ago. The other was barely a few days ago. That's all I know, I swear it."

Something made María push harder.

"I think you're still hiding something. So, tell me, 'cause if you don't, there's no deal."

Teodoro shuffled restlessly in his chair.

"Look, I'm ashamed. I've never seen anything like that in my life. I should have told you when you came to the funeral home"

"Well, tell me now."

"Well, it was a few nights ago. It was already late, but there was an early service the next morning, and I went downstairs to make sure that Peter had prepared the body properly, and oddly he hadn't locked the door like he usually does, and when I entered the room I almost died."

"What did you see, Teodoro?"

"Oh, you're not going to believe it! I saw Peter up on the table having sex with a dead woman."

Chapter 24: The Reptile

Day 15, Monday

Peter Raymond turned out to be an odd fellow. He moved apprehensively, like a lizard. Nevertheless, he was well dressed and well mannered. When Duquesne and O'Donnell came in the room, he stood up. They told him to take a seat, and he did so immediately.

María began to go over some papers in the folder that she was carrying. She knew that waiting a few minutes made some suspects more nervous, but it didn't seem to faze Raymond. *It must not be the first time that the police have questioned him, even though we haven't found any previous criminal record*, María thought.

They were with him for an hour. They confronted him with the details that Ted Light had given them, with the testimony of the witness that had seen the limousine take away Esmeralda Reyes, with the forensic information that they were likely to find in the vehicle and the funeral home. But Peter Raymond didn't say a word. They couldn't get him to open his mouth. It was only after María told him that they had found the body of the Nicaraguan woman that he said:

"I didn't kill her."

He repeated it three times, but it was the only words he uttered.

María looked at her watch. She left the room, and behind her O'Donnell.

"How long can you keep him here?"

"At least twenty-four hours."

"Okay. Throw both of them in the same cell and give me until tomorrow morning, maybe even sooner."

"Call me if you need anything, and at any hour if you find out something."

"You got it."

As soon as she got back in the car, she called Fernández who was on his way to meet her. She told him to wait for her at the station and to have the photo of Gregorio Antonio Ibarra on his tablet.

They went to the airport to wait for the painter at the Iberia gate. María and Fernández saw him as he came through the Immigration booth. She commented to her assistant:

"If my intuition hasn't failed me, that man knows something but he isn't guilty of anything. Maybe he has ice water in his veins because he looks perfectly calm to me."

They followed him closely. They watched him look at his phone while he waited for his luggage. They observed as an elderly woman spoke to him and pointed out her suitcase, and he courteously lifted it from the conveyor belt and handed it to her. By all aspects, it seemed to be a chance encounter and a kind gesture by the Spaniard, but the detectives didn't leave anything to chance. They slyly took photos of the woman and her suitcase.

As Ibarra left Customs with two trunks, they approached him. The man wasn't surprised. On the contrary, he commented:

"I'm glad to see you. I was going to go down to the station first thing tomorrow morning."

María asked him if they could go right then instead, and he agreed without hesitation.

As soon as the three of them got settled in, the man began to speak without them asking him a single question.

"Look, I read in the papers about the two murders, the one on Biltmore Way and the other at Vizcaya, and right away I remembered a couple of things that, I don't know, might be useful."

The two detectives listened anxiously.

"You're aware that I have a fellowship at the Vizcaya Palace. About a month or two ago—I'd have to check my calendar to give you the exact date—a strange man showed up at the studio. They don't tend to allow tourists into that area, and the few visitors we do have are generally accompanied by a guide or some Vizcaya employee. It's so that we can work in peace, and also I imagine they're concerned about someone stealing something."

There was a brief pause and then the man continued:

"In short, this man—who wasn't dressed too poorly, but had a strange look to him as if he were, I don't know, a reptile—waltzed in among the artists and started looking at everything. He stopped at each work. He was there about twenty minutes. He made me really nervous."

"And?" Fernández casually replied.

"He stopped to talk to me. He asked me about the piece I was painting. You know that I use a lot of elements of Francisco Goya in my work. I explained to the visitor that there was the most famous Goya— the one of the naked *Maja* and also the clothed one— and then there's the one of the Court, but also the ones of the beggars, the disasters of war, and the dark etchings. And today we were living in a similar

187

reality, one of great riches and enormous pockets of poverty, even in developed nations like Spain and the US."

As he spoke, Ibarra became excited. His honey-colored eyes shone brighter, and he moved his hands with adamant gestures, his fingers incredibly thin and delicate for a man of his size. Perhaps it was his accent, but something reminded María of her friend Joaquin del Roble. *I need to visit to Spain*, she told herself. Being in the middle of such a complex investigation, she was surprised that such an idea would pop into her head. Even more so, she thought about how she would like to go with David, and also her father and with Patrick; however, she knew that it was not only complicated to line up everybody's schedules, but it was difficult for people of such diverse tastes to travel together.

Ibarra was not getting to the point and Fernández intervened again:

"I'm going to show you several photos and you tell me if you recognize the man you're talking about."

"That one! That's him! He told me his name was Peter Raymond. Is that his real name?"

"We believe so. At least, that's the one he goes by. Tell us what happened after you spoke about your painting."

"At first, nothing. He told me he liked it a lot. He came back a few days later. Once again I was surprised, but since we're all a little vain I guess, and he came right to my easel, I felt special. This time he asked me how much my paintings were going for and if I had an agent or someone representing me. As for the latter I told him no, and I didn't want to confess that I hadn't sold a single painting in the United States. Obviously, I haven't had an exhibit or anything of the sort. My fellowship has just gotten underway, and I've used my time to rework my style because..."

Fearing that he'd go off on another tangent, this time it was María who got him back on track.

"So, what happened?"

"Well, on his third or fourth visit he told me that he knew a person that could set me up with a very successful representative. I told him that'd be great since I didn't have anything to lose. He came back a few days later with another man, who seemed serious, dressed in an expensive, designer tracksuit. They chose one of my paintings and told me that they would have to take it with them. I refused. I wasn't going to let two strangers walk off with one of my paintings. As a guarantee, they agreed to let me go with them since they were going to frame it first so it would look better. The three of us went to a type of warehouse. I'm not too familiar with Miami, but I paid attention because all of it was so weird. I know we took Route 1, not towards downtown but in the other direction. I believe we headed north, right? And then we took a right. I could see that the name of the street was Bird, and we went several blocks until we took a left where the avenues are numbered in the 70s. It was a very rundown neighborhood, not like the one around Vizcaya. They had a key to the warehouse. They took the painting to the back and began to frame it. They left me seated at a round table up front, and each time I insisted on seeing how the painting was coming along, they refused to let me, and said that it'd be better to see it once it was finished. They brought out a bottle and three glasses. They were coming and going. I heard hammering and some voices, but after three drinks I didn't care."

"Did you see anyone else? Did they tell you anything?"

"I didn't see anybody else, but based on the voices I was hearing, I'm pretty sure that there were others or, at least, one more. And yeah, the two of them came and sat down with me, and said stupid things about this and that. Now I think it was just to keep me busy."

"And what happened when they were done?"

"Well, before they finished something weird happened. Hell, now I think it should have set off some alarm bells with me, but I guess I had had too many drinks, and I just thought it was a joke maybe."

"What happened?"

"So this Peter guy began to tell me in a round-about way that he had an erotic fantasy and maybe I could help him. Shit, I immediately wondered if he was gay and was trying to pick me up? I got really nervous. I think he realized what I was thinking because he leaned back in his chair and confessed that he had dreamed about making love to a woman in the Vizcaya gardens, dressed like they did in the 1920s. I almost felt relief. He wanted me to help him sneak a woman in at night, but I told him I couldn't because I was there on a fellowship, and I would put my funding in jeopardy. And then he said something that I didn't think much about at the time, but after I read that about the woman who was found dead there, I can't get it out of my mind."

"What did he say?" asked Duquesne and Fernández at the exact same moment.

"I can't remember his exact words, but it was something like 'we won't make any noise. My little woman will be quieter than a stiff.'"

Neither of the two detectives showed any signs of surprise. María asked:

"What happened to the painting?"

"They wanted me to leave it there, but I refused. Then they made some calls and we went to a different area in Miami with expensive villas, wealthy people, and lavish plants. There in the parking garage of a condo we met an elegant and beautiful young woman. She had a prepared receipt for me. She told me that she'd try to sell the painting at a good price, and for me not to worry since all the great works of art that she stored in her apartment were insured. She brought a small dolly with her, which caught my eye since it was red, and then they placed the painting on it, covered it with a sheet, and strapped it down with some cords that she had brought with her. It was going to be impossible for the painting to fall off when they moved the dolly. It was on wheels, and she refused to let us go with her. She went up the ramp with no problem, unlocked a door, and left. Even though she seemed to be legitimate, I was left with a receipt in my hands and the impression that I'd never see my painting again, a single penny, or that woman who had disappeared like a ghost. But at the same time, I thought maybe this would be my big break to get into the US market since, after all, she was an American."

They showed him the photo of Sarah Turner, and Ibarra immediately identified her as the woman with the red dolly. Now they needed to find out who the man in the designer tracksuit was. For the moment, however, they had finally figured out which painting had been stolen from the apartment on Biltmore Way, and that the connection between the two murders was not only the painting but Peter Raymond, the man who seemed like a reptile.

Chapter 25: Tight Lipped

Day 16, Tuesday

The previous night, once Fernández had taken the Spaniard home, María called O'Donnell to fill him in on what she had found out about Peter Raymond. She agreed to come in the next morning to interrogate him.

Her cell phone woke her up early that Tuesday morning. As soon as she saw Keppler's name appear on the screen, she knew it was something serious.

"Have you seen the news this morning?"

"No."

"Well somehow the press found out about the business at the funeral home and it's caused a big scandal. Find out what's going on and come in as soon as you can."

Indeed, the local news channel had reported that the Broward Police had responded to accusations of irregularities at the Joseph Baker Funeral Home, and officers had been seen at the site. There were reports of bodies being buried alongside other corpses and of ashes mixed with those of other cremated bodies.

Clients were in the parking lot demanding answers, and the funeral home had been cordoned off with yellow tape as if it were a crime scene. When María saw that CNN was also running a story about it, she imagined that her friend O'Donnell must be going crazy. The same went for the owner of the funeral home, and they still didn't know whether he was an accomplice or if the employees had just pulled one over on him.

She took a quick shower. She stopped for a Cuban coffee because she knew she wouldn't last long without it. She was getting back in the car when the phone rang again. It was Fernández.

"Are you aware of the mess that's going on?" María asked him.

"Yes, but I'm calling about another matter. I just spoke with Susan Lanuza Brown, you know, the one from the firm that represents Anderson. She called asking for you."

"And?"

"Anderson's going to appear before the judge at 2:00 this afternoon. She wants us to talk to the prosecutor so that we don't object to him getting out on bail."

"I don't have a problem with that. That man didn't kill Sarah Turner and doesn't pose a danger to anyone. He has the money to pay a high bail, but I won't oppose it if they lower it. It's possible that we'll have to withdraw the charges before long."

"Since you signed the arrest order, you're the one who has to speak with the prosecutor. Do you want me to get in touch with him?"

"I'm heading that way, but I don't have the case number."

"Don't worry. I'll get all the information together, and you'll just need to get on the phone and tell him that you approve."

That's what they did. Fernández was very efficient, but María thought he seemed to take a special interest in this particular case. She made a mental note to ask him about it when the opportunity arose.

At the station, the telephones were ringing off the hook. Worse still, when she tried to head inside, the TV cameras surrounded her. Somehow, the press had learned that they had confiscated the limousine and that they too were working the case.

She repeated "no comment" a thousand times until she managed to get inside. She went directly to Keppler's office.

Her boss was fixated on finding out who had leaked the information to the press.

"Larry," she told him in a disarming tone, "it must have been someone from the Broward office. You know that no one here would do that. Besides, right now we're not going to get anywhere rehashing it."

"You're right. What we have to do is solve the two murders. Do you have any leads?"

María told him about the conversation with Ibarra and how certain she was that if Peter Raymond wasn't the murderer, he was at least involved in some way.

"Well, go interrogate him right away before they book him and the Feds don't grant you access to speak with him."

This time María took Fernández with her. She knew that he often managed to gain the confidence of suspects and get them to talk. On the way there, they poured over the case.

"I've got it. I know how to get this guy to talk," Fernández said reassuringly.

María let her partner go in the interrogation room with O'Donnell's assistant where Peter Raymond was waiting. She remained behind the two-way mirror and observed. She listened to Fernández who presented himself in a very relaxed fashion, as if he were at a bar or social get together. It surprised her what he led with:

"I suspect that you know a lot about movies. Better yet, it seems to me that you are very familiar with the films of D.W. Griffith."

With that, Peter Raymond began to pay attention.

"Personally, I think *Way Down East* was brilliant for its era. I don't know how many times I saw it. And you?"

Raymond still didn't take the bait.

"The scene with Anna Moore in the snowstorm was remarkable. Lillian Gish couldn't have done a better job."

María didn't have the slightest idea what Fernández was talking about, but Raymond obviously did. She saw how his face lit up.

"What I still can't figure out yet is who's more to blame: Lennox, who was rich and selfish; or Anna, who was naïve and believed his lies; or Martha—do you remember, the old town gossip?—; or Squire Bartlett who abandons Anna in the snowstorm after he learns of her past, right after she lost her child."

"Anna wasn't that big of an idiot," replied Raymond who had been glued to the story, which was completely unfamiliar to María but she knew it had something to do with the film's plot.

"Of course not, because she liked to sleep with Lennox."

"And his money. If he weren't rich, she wouldn't have paid any attention to him."

"Do you think so?"

"I know so. When you're dying from hunger, women don't even look at you."

"Is that how it is for you, Peter?" Fernández asked. María was afraid that Raymond was going to stop talking but he didn't.

"Look, there was a time when I had more than enough money, and I had all the women I wanted, but things went south for me, and they all turned their back on me. They're all bitches."

"Obviously. And that's why they need to be punished."

"I don't punish them."

"You've never killed a single one of them? I would understand it if you did. There are certainly times I'd like to."

Raymond looked at him amusingly, as if knew that Fernández didn't care for women.

"I've never killed anyone. I swear it."

"Then maybe you should tell us the truth about what you've done, or they're going to pin you with the murder of the dead woman at Vizcaya who was found lying in a pose just like Lillian Gish at the end of the film."

"But without the snow," Raymond clarified with a smirk.

"Without the snow, but it was cold. Corpses speak, Peter. You better start talking too 'cause in two hours the Feds are going to take you away and then we won't be able to help you any longer."

"And what type of deal can you give me if I do?"

"That depends on what you tell us."

"Look, I don't have anything to lose because I haven't done anything wrong. I'm just a man who believes in love beyond this life."

"That's what I was thinking. So, tell me the whole story, 'cause I'm very interested," Fernández lowered his voice so much he could hardly be heard.

"Look, it's not that unusual. It even has a name, necrophilia. I'm not the first. They even say that Achilles, the one from the Trojan War, did it. I've read about it. These days you can find everything on the Web. Man, I tell you. I love sleeping with dead women. Those women let you do anything and they never kiss and tell…"

"And that's what you did with Esmeralda Reyes?"

"Who's that?"

"The one you somehow snuck into Vizcaya."

"It was one of my fantasies that kept me up at night. To make love to a woman dressed in a costume from the 1920s in the Vizcaya gardens. And I did it! It was delicious."

María felt like she was going to gag but knew that Fernández had managed to get Raymond to confess because he was enjoying reliving the moment of his ecstasy. The truth is her partner never ceased to amaze her.

An hour later, Peter Raymond recounted how he had hidden drugs for some guys; that he had buried or cremated several women who they had brought in; and that throughout his career at various funeral homes in different states he had made love—as he described it—with many dead women.

"About how many would you estimate?" the detective asked him.

"Exactly one hundred. You don't believe me? I have them all written down."

Chapter 26: That Stupid Look

Day 16, Tuesday

When they got back to the station, María had three messages from Patricia Duarte, Eric Anderson Jr.'s first wife. She returned her call right away. The woman spoke calmly, but the detective could tell that she was nervous by the slight quiver in her voice.

"Officer Duquesne, we need to see you. My son Jack would like to speak with you."

"Are you in Naples?"

"No, here in Miami. At his Uncle Marty's house. Can you come by?"

"I'm on my way."

When Duquesne and Fernández knocked at the door of the house in Coconut Grove, they were surprised that not only was almost the entire family there, including Linda Astor Anderson, but also the lawyer Susan Lanuza Brown. The only ones missing were Mr. Anderson (the father), Elizabeth's husband, and the girls. Even Laura—Junior's current wife— was there. María realized that it wasn't going to be easy to question Jack with such an entourage present, and obviously the lawyer had thought the same thing.

"Well, we understand that you'd prefer to speak with Jack down at the station, but he's very nervous. Marty has offered us his study where we can meet and have a bit of privacy."

The two detectives, the lawyer, Patricia Duarte, and Jack headed into the study. The boy's eyes were red. María recalled what her own son was like at that age, and she couldn't help but feel a bit sorry. Before she could say anything to him, the young man broke down into tears. He kept repeating:

"I don't want my grandfather to go to jail. I don't want my grandfather to go to jail."

María waited until he regained his composure.

"Look, Jack, if you know something that can help your grandfather, you have to tell me. Why don't we start from the beginning? You knew Sarah Turner, right?"

"Yes, she was a friend of the family. I had seen her several times."

"And the Sunday before last, when you had a football game in Miami, did you go to her apartment?"

"I didn't kill her. I didn't kill her…" The young boy repeated as he sobbed interminably. The lawyer went to speak, but María made a gesture with her hand to stop her.

"Look, Jack, I have a son. He's a little older than you, but you remind me of him when he was your age. You have to trust me. Sometimes things happen that we don't intend to, by accident. If that's what it was, everything will be cleared up."

The young man seemed to calm down and was about to begin speaking when he once again began quivering as he sobbed.

"I didn't mean to. I didn't mean to…"

Once again, María waited. She saw the great anguish reflected on Patricia Duarte's face. She sensed that the woman was about to interrupt and put an end to the questioning.

"Jack, look me in the eyes. I don't have any other choice but to do my job and find out what happened. It'll be easier on all of us if you tell me what happened. Tell me. Why did you go see Sarah?"

"The thing is, I heard my father and grandfather talking."

"What were they saying?"

"That Sarah was going to have a baby, and they'd have to figure out a way to keep my grandmother and Laura from finding out."

"And what else did you overhear?"

"Dad was joking that what bothered him the most was that he was going to have to share more of the inheritance. My grandfather didn't think that was funny and told him not to talk like that."

"Was that all?"

"No. Before that, they were saying that it'd be better if she didn't have the baby, that there was still time to convince her, that being a career woman she probably wasn't that interested in being a mother."

"Anything else?"

"I don't know, because without meaning to, I made some noise. They saw me, and I acted like I had just come in. I believe they thought that I hadn't overheard anything."

"And when was this?"

"I don't know, about two weeks ago, one night when I slept over at my dad's house."

"And why did you go see Sarah? To ask her not to have the baby?"

"Sweetie, these are matters for adults. You're not old enough to understand such things," Patricia Duarte intervened.

"Oh, Mom, every one of my friends and I have lent money to somebody or another so they could pay for their girlfriend's abortion. I know a lot about these things. I even had the phone number of the doctor that could do it for them."

"And why didn't you want her to have it? I think there's plenty of money to go around in this family if need be," María regretted the comment as soon as she said it.

"I didn't care if I had a sister, but I didn't want a brother."

"Oh. And how did you get there? How did you get in?"

"I walked part of the way and took the Coral Gables trolley the rest. I went in through the main door just as a lot of people were going in."

"And what happened in Sarah's apartment?"

Jack took a deep breath.

"The door was already cracked open. I knocked and thought I heard some noise inside, like people speaking in a low voice and moving around. I thought maybe it was the television. Finally, Sarah showed up at the door and told me to come in. She was surprised to see me and offered me a Coke. I told her not to treat me like a kid, that I had come to talk to her about something serious."

"How did she react?"

"What angered me the most was that stupid look on her face, like she was laughing at me, as if she wasn't following what I was talking about. I explained, I begged, but nothing. She didn't move from where she was, and she didn't answer me."

"Was there someone else in the apartment? What happened next?"

"I don't know if anyone else was in the apartment. She watches the neighbor's cat sometimes, and I thought that maybe the cat was there. I'm not sure."

"And?"

"I got mad because she wouldn't answer me, and I went to shake her, but I barely touched her and she fell to the floor, and lay there like she was dead."

"And what did you do?

"I saw a raincoat on one of the chairs. I grabbed it, and put it on and took off running. The doorman must have confused me with one of her relatives because he yelled out 'Mr. Turner. Mr. Turner!' but I just kept on running until I ditched the raincoat and took the trolley again. Since then I haven't been able to sleep. I didn't mean to kill her. I swear it. I only grabbed her by the arms…"

Jack hugged his mother and began to bawl again.

"Just one more question, Jack. It's important that you tell me the truth."

"Did you leave her there on the floor?"

"Yes, but I barely even touched her."

María knew that Jack was telling the truth and that someone else had killed Sarah and left her on the bed after the young man had left, possibly someone who was already in the apartment when he arrived. But, who and why?

Chapter 27: Twenty Years Earlier

Day 17, Wednesday

The last thing María wanted to do that morning was to testify in court. It wouldn't have mattered if it had been any other day, but that strange felling she got in her chest was a sign that she was getting close to solving the two murders. It irritated her that she had to take time away from the investigation. On the bright side, she assumed that she would be one of the first witnesses called in the trial. She hoped that it wouldn't take too long.

Actually, it was an extraordinary case. The events had taken place almost two decades ago when she had just joined the police force. She was just a rookie. She and her partner had gone to a house as part of an investigation regarding the disappearance of a woman. The husband had reported that she had been missing for three days. Even though so much time had passed, her memory took her back to that morning and that modest, but clean and well-kept house; the American husband in an undershirt, drinking beer in front of the television; and the little boy, barely six-years-old, with his head down and crying his eyes out.

They had to take the father, who was indisputably intoxicated, down to the station to question him. Since they couldn't locate any relatives nearby, they called the agency that dealt with children in such cases so that they could come take care of the young boy temporarily. As they were taking him away, the young boy looked up at María and said to her:

"Dadda hurt Mommy."

María leaned down to his height and asked him to repeat what he had said since his pronunciation seemed a little garbled.

"Dadda hurt Mommy."

If she had had more experience, María would not have let them take the child away, rather she would have requested that a psychiatrist speak to him down at the station. Still, she thought it wouldn't matter, provided that they did it later.

Over the next few days, the police looked everywhere for Bonnie Darrell. She was a young woman, in her twenties, from Georgia. She wound up getting pregnant at sixteen and went to live with the baby's father. Both Bonnie Darrell and her partner, Michael Crowder, had criminal records for possession and consumption of drugs. The two incidents had occurred before the pregnancy and there wasn't any evidence of domestic abuse. When a neighbor, despite his doubtful credibility, suggested that Bonnie had taken off with a former boyfriend who had visited her recently, the police believed that she really had abandoned her husband and child. Besides, they didn't have leads to follow regarding her whereabouts and they closed the search. María presumed that no one had interviewed the young boy and that she should have insisted that they do so.

After little Mike, as he was called when he was younger, had been in the custody of the State for almost a year, the father gave up his rights, and a family from Georgia, precisely where his mother had been from originally, adopted him. Twenty years went by, and María found out later that the child had led a happy life, at least until a few months ago. He had just graduated from a vocational school to become an X-ray technician when his adoptive parents were killed in an automobile accident.

The young man carried out all the necessary procedures like a robot. He felt disoriented. He began to have nightmares and to recall images from his childhood that he didn't know he still remembered. For the first time in many years, he even started thinking constantly about his real mother, the one who had brought him into the world and who had disappeared when he was a child. He returned to Miami and found a job. When the opportunity to buy his childhood home arose, he decided to buy it with the money he had inherited from his adoptive parents. That small house reminded him of a time when his mother bathed him and dressed him, and made him his Cream of Wheat that he liked so much, where she played ball with him in the yard, and at night sang him beautiful songs. As for the father, he only had a vague memory, like a dark and threatening shadow that he preferred to keep at a distance. He presumed he was alive, but he didn't want to know anything about him.

Mike moved to his new house with feelings of nostalgia and hope. The neighborhood had improved but his house wasn't in good shape. He changed out the doors and windows, remodeled the kitchen and bathrooms, and painted it. Finally, he furnished it with great affection, and life went on its own way. He was happy at work, and he began to go out with a girl that he really liked. The pain from the unexpected death of his parents and the deep feeling of abandonment that he had felt was going away little by little. He decided it was time to spruce up the yard.

María had read all about his story in the press and had even seen part of an interview the young man had given on TV. The case was really sad.

When Mike began to dig a hole in the flowerbed to plant a tree, the shovel hit something hard. He discovered soon enough that it was a skull. He immediately called the police. It turned out to be his mother's dead body, the young lady who supposedly had abandoned him for an old boyfriend. With her bones before him, the young man bawled uncontrollably as he had never done before for his mother, perhaps because he had held onto the belief that she was alive. Perhaps he had even fixed up that old house with the absurd idea that she might return one day.

That morning María had to testify in the trial of Michael Crowder for the murder of Bonnie Darrell. After she swore on the Bible that she would tell the truth and sat down, she looked across from her at the defendant's bench, at that man whom she had only seen once before, drunk and in an undershirt, in front of a television at his house. Now he was fatter and almost bald, dressed in an impeccable suit and a recently bought tie. María also noticed a young man seated on the front row whom she recognized as Mike, that young boy with a round face and blond curly hair who had told her what she was now repeating to the prosecutor:

"Dadda hurt Mommy."

María realized that despite her testimony and the discovery of the body at the house where the couple had lived when Bonnie Darrell disappeared, the prosecutor still had to prove that the husband had killed her. It wasn't surprising that Mike's face reflected a great sense of anguish.

After she testified, María thought about staying until the court was in recess so she could go greet the young man, but she felt her cell phone vibrate. She went into the hall to answer it. It was Fernández.

"You're not going to believe what I've found out about Sarah Turner's friend—Betty—and her ex-husband."

"I'm on my way. I'll call you from the car."

While she was on her way to the station, Ivan Fernández got her up to speed.

"The telephone records show a bunch of calls between Betty and Tim Parker. I went over the building's entrance and exit videos for the days immediately prior to and after the murder, and there are several times it could have been Parker. I think you're right: there definitely is something fishy here."

"Anything else?"

"Yes, he has a case pending against him for fraud of an art work."

"Hmm."

"I haven't told you the best part. There was a cash deposit in one of her accounts for $15,000 two days prior to the murder and then another in the same amount three days later."

Chapter 28: The Kitchen

Day 17, Wednesday

María tried to organize her thoughts. Anderson had already posted bail and left the jail. She didn't want to arrest Jack. She was convinced that neither of the two were guilty. Could it have been Junior? And what if he left the country and went somewhere that didn't have extradition? They were very wealthy people and could even hire a private jet. Sarah Turner and her unborn baby deserved justice. Nevertheless, María was now under the impression that she had been wrong to presuppose that the murderer was a member of the powerful Anderson family. Her intuition—or her nose, as her father called it—which she had relied on so successfully throughout her career, was leading her in a different direction, especially now that she had heard the business about the painting from Ibarra and the information from Fernández about the calls between Betty and Sarah's ex-husband, Tim Parker.

When she got back to the station, she told Fernández that she wanted to go over the surveillance tapes from Biltmore Way. They started with the ones from the parking garage and the entrance at the side door. Indeed, they witnessed Sarah Turner with the little red dolly coming in with the painting by GoyA. They also saw footage from two different occasions that showed her friend Betty and a man who knew how to avoid the camera, but easily could have been Tim Parker. The last time they were seen gaining entrance to the property was on the Saturday before the murder. On early Monday morning, the camera caught sight of Betty with the little red dolly and a painting that she stashed in her car. She returned an hour later, only to leave again, accompanied this time by the man they suspected to be Tim Parker.

"Does Tim Parker have a criminal record? Are his fingerprints in any database?"

"They're not in the FBI or Miami databases. I've already checked with New York where he has that pending case, but I haven't gotten any word back yet. Besides, we'd need more proof because, just like with Betty, both of them can justify why their fingerprints would be in Sarah's apartment."

"Do we have any full-length photos of Tim Parker?"

"The one I took of him at the funeral only shows his face."

"I didn't take a single one. Everything happened so quickly. We could try to use the computer program to superimpose an image over another to see if they line up. I don't really know how to go about it, but I'm sure someone here does."

"I've been looking for his name in photos from painting exhibits in New York, but I haven't found anything yet. Do you think I should call Sarah's sister to see if she has a photo?"

"Yes... Wait a minute, no. Let's go to Sarah's apartment first, and casually go by Betty's. I don't want her to realize that she's a person of interest, so let's see how she reacts."

Sarah felt that same uneasiness that she did the first day when she visited that apartment, which was so organized and elegant but where the owner had been murdered. It was as if that inconsistency didn't line up with María's vision of the world, even though she had learned a long time ago that appearances could be deceiving. Fernández went directly to the nightstand. In response to the look that his boss gave him, he explained:

"This is where women hide their intimate secrets, right?"

Indeed, in the second drawer they found a small album with several photographs of Sarah Turner and

Tim Parker. Among them, there were a few from the courthouse in New York when they had gotten married. In the photographs, both of them were standing, so perhaps they could compare his appearance in the photos with the man on the security camera tape.

They also found the key to Betty's apartment, which earlier she had asked them to return. They knocked on her door.

"Hello, we've come by to return your key. Is this the one? I apologize for the delay."

Betty thanked them. It didn't seem like she was going to invite them in, but Fernández used his wits:

"Don't tell me you're making Cuban coffee! I can smell it! Hey, be careful. It sounds like it's about to boil over."

The woman reacted instinctively and ran to the kitchen with the detectives right behind her.

"Oh, I am so sorry, but a good cup of coffee is exactly what I could use at this hour of the afternoon. I hope you don't think I'm being too forward."

María knew that on occasion Fernández exaggerated his mannerisms so that his homosexuality would be obvious. This time she realized that it was an effective tactic. Many people, men and women alike, presumed him to be harmless.

Betty served them both their coffee and gestured for them to have a seat around the kitchen table.

"If it's okay with you, would you mind having your coffee in here?"

"On the contrary, kitchens are the heart of any home. I love them. I remember every single one of them in each house I have lived in. And yours is precious. I love how you've decorated it. It looks like you've remodeled it not too long ago. Those cabinets are the latest fashion. Did Sarah help you pick them out?"

It hadn't escaped María that Fernández had begun to speak to Betty in a chummy tone and had taken the conversation almost to a level of intimate friendship.

"Why yes, I just remodeled. No, Sarah was very busy and couldn't go with me to pick out the cabinets. Do you think they came out okay?"

"Oh, doll, they're divine."

While Fernández gushed on and on about the coffee and the recently remodeled kitchen, María took a look around, hoping to find something that would offer her a clue.

Finally, it dawned on her to ask:

"Betty, since you're in the art world, by chance have you ever heard of a Spanish painter who signs his work GoyA? You know, obviously not the famous Goya, but a contemporary painter."

Betty kept her composure, but María discerned a brief pause before she answered, as if she were weighing the consequences of the statement she was about to give:

"No, I don't think I've heard of him. Why?"

"It's not important. His name came up in connection to the murder at the Vizcaya Palace. He's there on a fellowship. Are you sure you haven't heard of him?"

"I don't think so…" There was a hint of anxiety in the woman's voice.

There was an awkward silence. At that very moment, María saw the notification on the screen of her cell that Keppler was calling, and the two detectives said a polite good-bye.

"I'm never going to forget that cup of coffee," Fernández told her as they took their leave.

María limited her comments to offering Betty her thanks.

Keppler had called to give them some urgent news:

"There's been an important development in the Vizcaya case. Get over here right away."

Chapter 29: Cross Stich

Day 17, Wednesday

The detectives had barely left the building on Biltmore Way and were getting in the car when María received a second call from Keppler.

"We're surrounded by the press here. You better head directly to the Broward station. O'Donnell's waiting for you."

"What's happened?"

"The DEA has made several arrests. It looks like it was a large operation, and it's possible that Esmeralda Reyes' murderer is among the ones they've arrested. It's important that you question him immediately. If you manage to get a confession, we might be able to charge him as early as tomorrow."

While Fernández drove, María searched the Internet for news. At times, the press was more up-to-date than the bulletins that came out from the police. She found out that they had raided a music recording studio in a shopping mall, a few doors down from a candy store that children often frequented. They had made the whole thing into a laboratory. They also found another lab in a private house very close to a school, this one with a machine capable of making five-thousand pills an hour. The worst epidemic in the country these days wasn't cocaine or heroin; it was opioids. The doctors prescribed sedatives like Oxycontin to relieve severe pain, and the opioids led to addiction. There were fake prescriptions and pills produced on the black market everywhere. It was estimated that thousands and thousands of Americans were dying annually due to overdoses, and the estimate was climbing.

The employees at the other stores near the music studio, as well as the neighbors near the residential house, never suspected anything. They were stunned when they found out that right next door to where they were working and living, they were manufacturing those infamous pills that could lead anyone to addiction and even death. It was rare to find someone who didn't know of a tragic case that involved someone's life being ruined or even cut short. Just a few days ago, on the front page of the newspaper there was a picture of a young man found dead in his car, parked in front of his house. He had turned eighteen that very day, and would have finished high school in just a few weeks. He in fact had just received word that he had gained admission to a prestigious university in Lexington, Virginia. They were investigating whether the boy had taken the drugs voluntarily or if someone else had slipped them into something he was drinking. Sometimes drug dealers did that type of thing to get kids hooked and to increase their buyers.

"Have you found out anything about the murderer?"

Fernández' voice jolted María out of her thoughts, which inevitably kept leading her to Patrick and the dangers he faced.

"No, they don't say anything about the murder, only that they've found two laboratories where they were making drugs."

The Broward County station in Hollywood was a beehive of journalists and photographers outside and federal agents and other officials inside. Fortunately, O'Donnell came out to meet them as soon as they came through the door, and took them to his office.

"So, María, I think we've arrested the person responsible for the death of Esmeralda Reyes, and I don't know how many others. We've made nine arrests, six men and three women. They're members of an international cartel and obviously the Feds are about to take them away. Let's get in there so you can question her and maybe find out at least what happened and get a few clues about the Sarah Turner case."

When María followed O'Donnell into the interrogation room, she was surprised to find a woman of indeterminable age and who had a look of defiance. María immediately felt like she knew her or at least had seen her face somewhere before.

The detectives had barely sat down at the table and María, as she usually did, had just started to go over the case file when the woman spoke up:

"I'm willing to tell you everything in exchange for immunity and that you offer me a new identity and protection."

Either this woman must be important or she's pulling our leg, María thought to herself. She looked at her once more and suddenly realized that she was the niece of an infamous drug lord from the 1980s, one of the founders of the Mexican drug empire. The woman, who had been beautiful in her youth, had attended college and married a police chief who wound up getting involved in drug trafficking. When a hitman, who had been hired by a rival cartel, riddled her husband with bullets, the young woman lost her way. They had nicknamed her the "Queen of the Pacific." She was arrested in a sting operation and pled guilty to aiding and abetting her husband, alias

"The Lion." She spent five years in prison and had been out for six. Her name was Sandra Alvarez Flores, and with her dark skin and green eyes, she was still very attractive even now in her forties.

"So, go ahead, speak," María told her.

"Not without a guarantee in writing first."

"I can't do that without knowing what you're going to tell me. If you don't want to talk, well, then first thing tomorrow morning you're going before the judge on charges of having murdered Esmeralda Reyes."

The woman thought about it.

"I'll tell you what I know if you give me your word that you'll get me a deal."

"The only thing I can promise you is that if you give us useful information, I'll try my best."

"You seem to be trustworthy. I am too. I think as woman to woman we can trust each other."

"So, tell me."

"I didn't kill that woman. Quite the opposite. I tried to save her. She came here as a 'mule' and was carrying balloons packed with cocaine in her stomach. They're so greedy that they sometimes fill the condoms too full—that's what they use, you know—and they break open since they can't tie a good knot in them if they're that full. They often lose the courier and the merchandise she's carrying. This time the girl didn't die, but the drugs that she had in her bloodstream made her sick and she had become irrational. When I got to the house where they were keeping her, she was unconscious and a doctor that they use for these types of things had opened up her stomach to take out the balloons that they could still salvage. Her blood was everywhere. I think they would have let her bleed to death, but I kicked all of them out, everybody except for that quack. I helped him stop the bleeding, and I began to sew her up. I was by her side for several hours, but it was useless. Regardless, she died. But I swear, I tried to save her."

"How can I be sure you're telling me the truth? Are you a nurse?"

"No, although in this business you learn a little bit of everything, and also from my mother, who taught me how to embroider when I was a kid. You can ask the medical examiner. I used a cross stich to embroider the top end of the stomach. Certainly, you're not going to think that just anybody would know that level of detail."

María remembered that Dr. Erwin had mentioned something to that effect, but in any case, replied:

"I'll look into it, but in order to offer you immunity and protection you're going to have to give us more than that."

"And I will. I can tell you about an entire network of narco-traffickers. I'm tired and ready just to have a normal life, but you have to protect me. If you don't, they'll kill me."

To María it seemed like she was dealing with a protagonist from a film or a Netflix series. She had never had a case like this. She turned around to look at O'Donnell and sensed that he was as perplexed as she was. She stood up:

"We'll see what we can do," she told the woman with green eyes.

Twenty-four hours later, the prosecutor had the agreement ready. Dr. Erwin carefully reviewed the photographs taken at Esmeralda Reyes' autopsy, and he could visibly make out the cross stiches that had been used to close up her stomach. The drug ring she told them about was without comparison. Among the thirty-seven arrested in Florida was their so-called doctor. All of them, and not one of them in particular, had killed Esmeralda Reyes, who had travelled to the United States with the dream of a better life.

Chapter 30: 305

Day 18, Thursday

Even before Dr. Erwin granted permission for Esmeralda Reyes' body to be released to her family, María had already managed to procure funds from a charity group that had been established years ago to assist with the funeral costs of victims without relatives or families with limited means. Dying in the United States—maybe everywhere—costs a lot of money. When she delivered the check to Esmeralda's son, she also gave him a business card from some friends who ran a funeral home.

"Look, they'll give you a good price here. Let me know when the viewing or burial is. I'd like to attend."

The young man showed his appreciation. The detective wanted to attend the final farewell not only to show solidarity with the relatives but also because murderers or their accomplices, or even witnesses that wouldn't dare speak to the police, sometimes made a discreet appearance at the funeral.

That morning, Esmeralda's mother, whom María had not spoken to before, called to tell her that the service would take place at Kingdom Hall that evening at 7:00, and she gave her directions. She told her not to feel obliged to come but that her grandson in particular was hoping to see her.

"He doesn't share the same faith as I do, and it's been difficult for him to cope with his mother's death. He wasn't opposed to me organizing a service in keeping with my religion."

María suddenly remembered that the grandmother was a Jehovah's Witness. She assured her that she'd be there at 7:00.

The detectives asked to see Mr. Anderson and his grandson Jack together. María wanted to avoid having the boy come in to the station. Once again, the meeting would take place at Marty's house. On the way to Coconut Grove, María abruptly asked Fernández:

"I don't know if I'm mistaken, but it seemed to me that you were rather deferential with the lawyer. What was her name?"

"Susan Lanuza Brown."

"Had you met before?"

"No, but I'm intrigued by her last name."

"Why?"

229

"Because José Antonio González Lanuza was an eminent Cuban lawyer in the early 1900s. He supported the War of '95, was taken prisoner in Ceuta, and later went into exile in New York. He wrote the first penal code in Cuba. He was very renowned, despite dying at a very young age."

"Fernández, how do you know all these things?"

"Because I'm curious and I read a lot. I'm interested in everything, especially everything that has to do with Cuba. I'm obsessed with it. Besides, in this case González Lanuza's father was a Galician immigrant like my great-grandfather. He was from Lugo and my relatives from Pontevedra."

"And the lawyer is a descendant of the famous barrister?"

"Yes, I think she's his great-granddaughter. She wound up taking off the González part, but after she married an American, she didn't want to lose the Lanuza surname. Apparently, it was her great-grandfather's story that inspired her to go into law. She's a good lawyer."

"Wow. How interesting. I don't know why, but when I think of Cuba the first thing that always comes to mind is everything that happened during the Revolution and then, secondarily, is the beauty of its scenery and beaches."

"There isn't another comparable to Varadero."

"You too Ivan? I thought that was a sentiment that you only heard from my father's generation."

"I'm teasing. But, in all honesty, it's the prettiest beach I've ever seen."

"Well, what I was saying was it had never dawned on me that Cuba was a country with penal and civil codes, and so many other things I'm unaware of."

The conversation was interrupted when they arrived at Marty's house. As they had requested, Mr. Anderson and his grandson were there. Also present were Jack's parents—Junior and Patricia—and the lawyer as well as the owner of the house, who upon their arrival offered them something to drink.

Fernández asked for some water, and Marty immediately handed him a plastic bottle. María wondered if Linda Astor Anderson would have approved of such manners, serving him without a glass, a saucer, or even a napkin. She thought she noticed that as Marty handed Fernández his water that their fingers brushed together and that the touch went on longer than necessary.

You're always seeing things that aren't there. If you hadn't known that they were gay, you would have never thought that. You just can't avoid your prejudices, María scolded herself mentally.

She asked Marty if she and Mr. Anderson, the lawyer, and Fernández could head to the study. The rest of the family remained in the living room.

"So, Mr. Anderson, you're aware that lying to the police is a crime. I know that you have wanted to protect your grandson, but he has already confessed, so it'd be best if you tell us the truth."

Eric Anderson acknowledged that Patricia and Jack had shown up at his house one night, both of them crying. The young man told him the same story that the detectives already knew. He felt responsible and guilty for his grandson going to prison, so without overthinking it he went to the police and turned himself in.

"Please! He's only a child," Anderson begged.

María thought about how despite all the money a family might have, nothing could protect them from life's problems. At that very moment, this millionaire was only a distraught grandfather, who knew that when it came to the law his fortune only served to let him hire a good lawyer. That was definitely an advantage, but it didn't solve the predicament they were in.

Susan Lanuza Brown intervened:

"It's our hope that Jack is charged as a minor."

"You know that's not up to me, but the D.A."

"You haven't even arrested him yet."

"No. And I'm not going to today, as long as Mr. Anderson gives me his word that neither his son nor grandson will leave the country."

Anderson seemed surprise:

"I promise you, but…"

María recognized that maybe she shouldn't show her cards, but at the same time it saddened her to see the anguish that the family was enduring.

"Look, Jack told us the truth. Just as he does, I too believe that he didn't kill Sarah Turner, that maybe someone else did after he left. If I can manage to make an arrest soon, everything will go better for him."

María sensed the relief that her words brought to Mr. Anderson.

"Go comfort your family, but what I've told you is confidential. You can't repeat it or you might hinder the investigation."

María decided against questioning Jack once more. She came up to him and said:

"Don't worry. You have a family that loves you a whole lot and they are here to help you. This nightmare is going to be over soon, you'll see."

When they were on their way back, Fernández chided her in an affectionate tone:

"Oh, boss, when it comes to children, you can't help but let your mother's heart bleed for them."

María knew that it was true and she didn't respond. On the way back to the station, she received a call from her father.

"I'm with Fernández in the car, *Papi*. You're on speaker," she cautioned him, although she knew her father would never say anything inappropriate.

"Well hello to Ivan. *Mi hija*, are you okay? I haven't seen neither hide nor hair of you."

"Yes, *Papi*. I'm sorry, but we've had a hard time keeping up with the two murders over the past few weeks. We've got one solved, and I think we have some good leads on the other one."

"I'm glad. I'm sure neither you nor Ivan have been eating well. If you have time to stop by, I've got a nice surprise."

Fernández bowed out, but he urged María to accept his invitation. He dropped her off at Patricio's house at 3:00 in the afternoon and agreed to come back for her at 6:15 so they could attend Esmeralda Reyes' funeral.

Her father met her at the door with a very cold Corona with a slice of lime in it.

"Oh, *Papi*, you're the best."

"Come on in. You're not going to believe what I have for you. Look, turns out there's a new little place on Bird Road, nothing less than a croquette bar! You can't believe the variety they have. I ate lunch there and bought several for you hoping you'd come by today. These are made with ham, and the ones here, that they call *305*, have ground beef and sweet plantains in them and they are a veritable delicacy."

As her father was speaking, he had already started to heat up the croquettes in the microwave, and then he served María who was sitting at the kitchen table enjoying her beer.

"What type of chips do you want with them? Plantain or cassava?

"Either one's fine, *Papi*. Well, cassava."

María gobbled it down while her father watched her affectionately.

"That was so delicious."

"Would you like some dessert? A cup of coffee? Or do you want to go rest up in your chair?"

"If I fall asleep, wake me up in an hour."

"I promise boss!"

She dosed off almost immediately, but not before thinking how wise her father was and how well he knew her. Patricio was dying for her to tell him all about the case, but he didn't ask her a single thing. His daughter would fill him in when she was ready.

Chapter 31: The Key

Day 18, Thursday

María and Fernández arrived at the Kingdom Hall of Jehovah's Witness on 34th Street Northeast at 6:45. It was a substantial two-story building, painted light pink with very few windows and white decorative bars. A high fence with railings enclosed the entire property and a parking lot, which was half-full. The two entrance gates were open and cars kept coming in.

They were walking toward the main entrance when they saw Aura getting out of her car—the Nicaraguan woman who cleaned Sarah Turner's apartment and who had found her dead. As they approached her, she seemed happy to see them. She immediately wanted to know if there were any new developments. In turn, they asked her why she was there.

"I was friends with Esmeralda Reyes," she said in a quivering voice, "and also her mother. She cleans several apartments in the Biltmore Way building and Esmeralda used to help her, that is, until they didn't renew her visa and she couldn't come back. Señorita Betty was going to help her get it renewed, but..."

"And how did she get to know Betty?"

"Because her mother cleans her apartment and, as I was saying, sometimes Esmeralda helped her."

The two detectives realized that they had found another link between the two crimes.

They entered the hall right before 7:00. It was almost full. María was surprised that a family of modest means would have so many friends until she realized that many in attendance were merely acquaintances whom they knew as members of the congregation. On the front row, they saw Robert—Esmeralda Reyes' son—with a young woman at his side whom María assumed was his wife and an older woman who was more than likely the grandmother—the victim's mother. The two detectives discreetly sat near the rear so they could see everyone who came in.

A few minutes after 7:00, a man took the microphone and began to speak. While she was carefully observing people in the audience and their movements, María listened to fragments of his sermon.

"Jesus said, 'I am the resurrection, and the life. He that believeth in Me, though he were dead, he shall live.'"

Other scriptures were less comforting:

"Wherefore, as by one man sin entered into the world, and death through sin, thus death too passed upon all men, for all have sinned."

The congregation listened in silence, as if in shock.

"But in keeping with his promise we look forward to a new heaven and a new earth, where righteousness dwells."

María thought she recognized someone she knew near the side doors.

At that moment, everyone stood and began to sing:

"Saul and Jonathan, beloved and pleasant in their lives…"

María nodded to Fernández to take a look over at the door on the right.

"…and in their death they were not parted…"

"Don't take your eyes off of her, and follow me without making a sound."

The singing continued:

"Swifter than eagles they were, stronger than lions."

"Don't make a sound. Come with me, please," María indicated to Betty, Sarah Turner's neighbor and supposed friend.

The woman didn't put up any resistance. As soon as they had exited the building, María told her that she'd have to go down to the station with them.

"Where's your car? In the parking lot?"

"No, out there, on the street."

"In case you needed to make a quick getaway, right?"

Betty didn't answer. María was certain that she had been involved in Sarah's murder, but she didn't have enough proof to arrest her, and even if she did she would undoubtedly get a lawyer right away. The best thing to do was to let her speak. Actually, the two detectives didn't have to work at it to get her to talk. In fact, she blurted things out so quickly that at times it was hard to follow the thread of what she was saying.

"I swear to you, I never thought that Sarah was going to wind up dead nor that I'd find myself in this mess either. You have to believe me. I always obey the law; I don't even go over the speed limit. It all began when Sarah and Tim Parker—you know, her ex—started having problems. Sarah and I weren't really close friends back then, and Tim would come by my apartment to have a glass of wine when she kicked him out. At the beginning, he was just a rejected husband looking to vent about his troubles.

He never said bad things about her or anything really. I don't even remember now what all he used to say."

"And then?"

"After he moved back to New York I didn't hear from him for a long time, and Sarah and I became good friends. But one day he just showed up at my door, just like that. I wish I had never let him in. He can be charming. He knows how to seduce a woman. We began to have an affair. I didn't think that there was anything wrong with it; Sarah didn't love him anymore. I would never sleep with one of my friend's husbands."

"How long ago was that? What else happened?"

"It wasn't that long ago, maybe a month and a half before Sarah's death. One day he started telling me about how important it was for him to buy this painting by Goya, but he needed money. I thought he was going to ask me for it, so I was apprehensive; but at the same time, I didn't think he was too serious because a Goya costs a load of money and no individual could possibly afford it. However, it turns out that it was by another painter, a contemporary artist who signs his work in the same way but with a capital "A" at the end. You know who I'm talking about because you asked me about him. I was scared and lied to you because I was worried. So, then Tim told me that Sarah had the painting, and he wanted to see it, take some photos, and that was all. You know how it is: he told me all of this in the middle of telling me how great I was and how much he loved me. I was so stupid! From the very beginning, all he wanted to do was use me. In a nutshell, he knew that I had a key to Sarah's apartment, and he asked me to let him borrow it. I refused. A few days later he told me that Sarah wasn't speaking to him and that she was going to get into a lot of trouble because there were drugs hidden in the frame of the painting and that they were going to send them to who knows where? Stupid me, I offered to go explain things to Sarah, but he convinced me that would only make things worse. A little later, he assured me that he had to steal the painting from Sarah's apartment, or they were going to kill both of them, and that if I helped him, he would give me $30,000. I didn't take him seriously because I didn't think it was possible that he'd have that kind of money, but two days later he deposited half of it into my account. He told me that by accepting it I was now implicated and a lot of other things that frightened me."

At that very moment Betty paused, hid her face in her hands, and seemed like she was about to break down crying. But she lifted her head, took a sip of water, and kept on going:

"Believe me, I never meant for anyone to get hurt or to get involved in something like this. I don't know why I didn't call the police. How could I have been such an idiot?"

"Tell me, what led to Sarah's death?"

"I finally gave in and lent him my key. He told me he would only go in when Sarah wasn't home. I wanted to make sure that was the case, so I went with him. I knocked on the door, convinced that she wasn't going to be there, and when she didn't answer I would leave, and let him go in. But, to my surprise, Sarah opened the door. I couldn't think of a single thing to say other than I was dying for a glass of wine and I didn't have any at my place. She invited me in. She asked me if I wanted to take a bottle back with me or if I just preferred to have a glass or two with her. I was speechless. I went in and, somehow, when she turned to go to the kitchen, Tim snuck in without her seeing him. A moment later, she came back to the living room with a bottle and two glasses. She poured the wine, but before she sat down, she excused herself saying that she needed to go to the bathroom for a moment. Tim came out of his hiding place and put some powder in her wine glass. With my eyes, I made a face telling him not to do it, but I couldn't say anything out loud or she'd know something was going on. He made a gesture like it was only going to make her fall asleep. Once again, I had the opportunity to warn her, but I didn't. My God, why? She had barely drunk half the glass when the doorbell rang. When she went to answer it, I realized that whatever Tim had given her was already taking effect because she was walking very slowly. I got up with my glass of wine and went and hid in the hallway."

"Was it Jack Anderson who was at the door?"

"Yes. I don't know him, but I've seen photos. Anyway, I hardly saw him. I only heard what he was telling Sarah. She didn't answer him. I think by that point she could barely stand on her own two feet. From what I could tell the boy became angry and was about to shake her by the shoulders, but he hardly touched her, and she collapsed. I saw him take a raincoat that was near the door, I don't know who it belonged to, and he took off running."

"What happened then?"

"I knelt down and could tell that she was alive but unconscious. Tim came out of his hiding place and told me to help him take the GoyA painting out. We were almost out the door with that huge canvas, but just then Sarah came to and began to scream. Tim left me holding the painting, and he went over to where she was. I'll never forget the expression of fear and surprise on Sarah's face. Underneath his jacket, he was wearing a tool belt, and he took out a hammer. He struck her one time in the head, so hard that I'm sure he killed her instantly. I didn't know what to do. I dropped the painting and ran over to where she was. I checked to see if she had a pulse. I should have called 911. I told him that we couldn't leave her there like that, just sprawled out on the floor. At my insistence, we placed her on the bed."

"Did you do anything else?"

"Yes, I covered her up. I don't why. She was dressed."

Once again, Betty lowered her head. It was clear that she was making a big effort not to break down.

"Ever since then I can't sleep. I'm almost relieved to be here. I couldn't keep it secret any longer. I've thought about going to the police several times, but Tim had threatened me."

"What happened then, that day, immediately afterwards?"

"We got the damn painting out of there, and we took it to my apartment. Two days later, Tim finally came for it. I haven't seen him since."

"He took it away, or you helped him?"

"Well, yes, I helped him."

"And where did the two of you take it?"

"I don't know. It was like some warehouse around 70th Avenue or so, before you get to Palmetto, south of Bird Road."

"You haven't seen or spoken with Tim again?"

"No, and I don't want to see him."

"But he did, in fact, deposit money into your account."

"Yes, but I never planned on spending it."

"And do you know where Tim, the painting, and the drugs are?"

"No."

"It would be smart if you cooperated with us because we're going to arrest you as an accomplice to murder."

Betty remained quiet for a moment.

"I might be able to help you find Tim Parker, but in exchange ..."

María knew that Betty was going to try to negotiate a reduced sentence in exchange for information. She was tired of making deals. It would be better for Betty to spend the night in jail, and then tomorrow she could take up the fight again. She left.

On the way home, her cell phone rang:

"*Mami*, I'm at the airport here with my suitcases. Are you going to come get me, or should I call *abuelo*, or take an Uber?"

The voice of her son brought her back to her life, her home, and all the things she loved.

"I'm on my way *mijo*."

Chapter 32: The Puzzle

Day 19, Friday

Even though she had stayed up late listening to Patrick's stories about his adventures in China, María got up early. A shower and a Cuban coffee at the stand she frequented allowed her to arrive at the station in a good mood. She felt that the arrest of Sarah Turner's murderer was imminent. All the pieces of the puzzle were coming together and were beginning to reveal the events that had led to the deaths of two women, who were very different but had the same right to live. Before long, she would only need to tie up the loose ends.

It didn't take much effort to find Tim Parker. A significant number of police officers had infiltrated the drug cartels. One of them said that Parker was in Orlando and was going to meet up with an undercover agent in a parking lot to sell him a bunch of Oxy-Contin, valued at $2,000. He would be surrounded by at least ten officers and they'd take him prisoner once the transaction was complete. María warned the agent that Parker had committed a murder so that they would arrest him upfront. They didn't pay attention to her. The sting almost cost the officer his life because he hadn't counted on Parker's accomplice putting a semiautomatic pistol a few inches from his heart. He handed over the money, but as soon as the car took off, a shootout started. By the time it was over, five officers had been injured and Parker and his accomplice lay dead a short distance from a preschool and not too far from where thousands of people of all ages were enjoying the enchantment of Disneyworld.

The charges against Eric Anderson had already been dropped, but it was still to be determined if there would be any against Jack. That afternoon the young man, his parents, and his lawyer met with the prosecutor. Despite her busy schedule, María managed to attend, and she was glad she did. The lawyer presented her case with legal arguments and just the right amount of compassion for the young man who was just beginning his life. The prosecutor agreed not to charge him under the condition that he undergo psychiatric treatment for six months and appear before the judge one more time to close the case. The proceedings would be sealed and would not appear as part of the young man's record.

The face of each member of the Anderson family showed great relief. María even thought that she noticed a gesture of mutual affection between Junior and Patricia, his first wife. *Having a child together is a connection for the rest of your life*, she thought, and was pleased that Bill and she were getting along so well. It was best for Patrick.

"Congratulations. You did a good job," María told Carmen Lanuza Brown. "Your great-grandfather would have been proud."

The young woman's face lit up:

"You know who my great-grandfather was?"

María wasn't good at lying. Even the little white lies that everyone tells got stuck in her throat.

"My colleague Fernández spoke to me about him. I thought that it was interesting that he wrote Cuba's first criminal code."

"I have a copy. It's fascinating. If you'd like…"

The conversation was cut short when the Andersons made their way over to thank them both for having helped Jack. Junior took María discreetly by the arm and when they were apart from the others, he asked her if she knew who the father of Sarah's baby had been.

"No, but the results should be in soon. I can only reveal them to her family and the father."

She made a mental note to call Dr. Erwin on Monday morning to check on the paternity test. They were comparing the baby's DNA to that of Eric

Anderson. If it was the son rather than the father, it would be sufficiently similar to ask for a sample from Junior, but at this point, it was probably better not to know.

María wanted to finish work early and start enjoying the weekend with her family, but she headed back to the station to make sure that she could inform Sarah Turner's family that the woman's ex-husband turned out to be the murderer and that he had paid for it with his life. When she spoke to Colleen, the young woman remarked:

"My mother told you so back in the beginning. Remember?"

She also called Gregorio Alberto Ibarra and told him that they had found his painting in a warehouse, but that they had to hold it as evidence. He had been cleared from any suspicion.

"Don't worry, Duchess. 'More than that was lost in Cuba.'"

Great, now there's another one who calls me Duchess, María thought to herself. She had heard the phrase "*more than that was lost in Cuba*" many times before, and for a long time she had presumed that it referred to the properties confiscated during the Cuban Revolution. Her father however explained to her that the phrase originated when the Spanish

Crown, despite all its efforts, failed to maintain control over the island, the last colony of an empire where the sun never set.

Betty had been released on bail, but the charges against her were still pending.

Keppler called María and Fernández into his office to congratulate them for having solved both cases.

"Take the rest of the week off," he told them.

"Thanks a lot. It's already Friday," they both replied in unison.

Even though she was in a hurry to get home, María accepted Fernández' suggestion that they go out for a beer to celebrate.

In silence, they sipped from their respective bottles of Corona, but all of a sudden, they both began to speak at the same time, going back over every detail they had lived during the past three weeks. María finally looked at her watch and realized that more time had gone by than she had planned.

Before leaving, spontaneously, she told Fernández:

"If you want to, come have lunch with us on Sunday. I'll text you the details. And, thanks for everything Ivan."

Chapter 33: The End?

Day 20 and 21, Saturday and Sunday

María was almost glad that Patrick was going to go out with his friends Friday night, and that he was going to sleep at Bill's and spend almost all day Saturday with him. As for David, he usually spent time with his kids when they were in Miami. She was in high spirits, almost euphoric, and would have liked to celebrate the close of both cases; instead, she had a light supper, put on her nightgown, jumped into bed, turned on the TV, and collapsed. She woke up ten hours later on Saturday morning like a new person.

She spent the day doing housework… well, so-to-speak. For some time, she'd had a cleaning lady come in every two weeks. The truth is that her townhouse in Doral didn't get very dirty. She was hardly ever home, so her bedroom and bath, den, and kitchen just required a mere tidying up more than a deep clean. She got busy going over the mail that had piled up, throwing out a bunch of things, cleaning and folding laundry (to her surprise Patrick had already done his dirty laundry from the trip), and then she went to the store. Tomorrow was Easter, and her family, David's, and some friends always came to her house for lunch. It was a tradition, just as they did for Thanksgiving at David's house. María liked traditions. They reassured her that there was still a rational order to life despite the many horrors and absurdities that she had to confront in the world of crime. Perhaps for that reason, before heading to the store she went by the cemetery and placed flowers on her mother's grave and even went into the chapel for a while. She remembered how her mother always bought a new dress for the occasion and would say:

"On Easter Sunday, one has to wear something new."

It seemed like she could still her voice. María continued her tradition, as if not doing so would have been a betrayal to her mother.

The weather on Sunday was splendid. It was sunny with a mild Lenten breeze typical of that time of the year, and not too hot. They could eat outside on the patio, which María had redecorated a few months earlier. With the new furniture, she could seat twelve at the table and the house didn't get dirty. She often liked to sit there outside and listen to the chimes, which were more intense during these windy days. María loved a neighbor's explanation that in Argentina they referred to wind chimes as "angel callers."

Her father was the first one to arrive. He had insisted that the two of them make their famous chicken and rice dish that they always prepared together, even though David was bringing an entire ham and sweet potatoes because the younger generation liked to follow American customs. Still, that didn't keep them from stuffing themselves with Cuban food.

A little after 1:00 everyone started to arrive, first David and his sons, then Patrick with a friend, and a bit later Fernández. They were all in a good mood. Lunch was delicious. The boys had fun talking about the adventures they had shared on their trip to China. It had been a long time since María had felt so relaxed and happy. Being together with her family brought back some internal peace. The stress from the weeks before was vanishing little by little with each sip of her beer, the sounds of the domino tiles, her father's voice, her son's laughter, and David's arms that gently squeezed her around the waist.

The main headline in that morning's paper dealt with a story about a drug trafficking ring, a shootout in Orlando, and the death of a painter from New York wanted for the murder of Sarah Turner. María had glanced at it. Now everyone was asking María and Fernández to share with them all the details about the case, but she didn't want to ruin the day:

"Please, I don't want to think about work today. I'll tell you some other time."

She was surprised that Fernández interrupted her:

"I want to tell all of you, but especially Don Patricio, that you should be very proud of María. She's an excellent detective, and she's taught me a lot."

"Come on, it's not that big of a deal, and besides I've learned so much from you. *Papi*, you should talk to him; he knows as much about Cuba as you do."

Around 5:00, Yolanda and Lourdes came by to drop off some chocolates. Even though they said they could only stay for a minute, they sat down at the domino table and stayed for an hour.

María snuck off to her room to escape the noise and called Joaquin del Roble.

"I didn't want you to think I had forgotten about you, Don Joaquin. I just…"

"No worries. I've already read about it in the paper and know you've scored a big success."

"Well, not really."

"This morning your boss was on TV and had wonderful things to say about you and another officer."

"That's the first I've heard about it."

"It was on a program on ABC, with Michael Putney. You know which one I'm talking about? At 11:30 in the morning. I just happen to catch it, but it made me so happy. Thank you for giving me a call, María."

"I promise I'll come see you soon. Take care of yourself, please."

"You know what the best medicine is."

"Of course. I'll come by one of these afternoons with a bottle of whiskey. I promise."

Around 7:00 people started leaving. Patrick asked María if she minded if he went out with Davicito and some other friends. She was relieved because in that secret language understood among couples, David had let her know that he planned to spend the night, and she felt uncomfortable making love when her son was in the house.

As soon as the two were alone, without even throwing away all the disposable glasses scattered around, the couple happily went to bed. Little by little, with each of David's caresses, María felt the accumulated tension leave her body and give way to pleasure.

They remained embraced for a long time, without speaking, half-asleep. She enjoyed immensely what some call 'love after love,' that special intimacy shared by couples who are not only in love but who truly understand each other.

The sound of her cell phone interrupted a moment when she felt genuinely happy. She was surprised to see Keppler's name on the screen.

"Mariita, I'm so sorry to bother you. You deserve a few days off, but…"

"What's the matter?"

"There's been a murder."

María got out bed.

"Does it have anything to do with the other cases?"

"No, I don't think so, not in the least."

"Where was it? Do you want me to go over to the crime scene?"

"Not this minute. Tomorrow. Your passport is up to date, right?"

"Yes. Why?"

"A Florida resident has been murdered in Cuba and I need you in Havana tomorrow without delay."

"But…"

"No 'but's' about it. Mario Conde will be waiting for you at the José Martí International Airport."

"But I've already told you before! Mario Conde is a literary character!"

"Oh, how would I know, María? I'll never understand that country in a million years, but there's no other alternative. You're leaving for Cuba tomorrow."

Author's Bio

Uva de Aragón (Havana, 1944) has published more than a dozen books of essays, poetry, short stories, and the detective novels *El milagro de San Lázaro (2017*) translated into English by Jeffrey C. Barnett and Kathleen Bulger-Barnett as *The Miracle of Saint Lazarus* (2019) and *El crimen de Biltmore Way* (2020). Her most recent book *El reino de la infancia. Memorias de mi vida en Cuba* (2021) won a Florida Book Award. Her first novel *Memoria del silencio* (2002), translated by Jeffrey C. Barnett and published as a bilingual edition by Cubanabooks in 2015, received second place from the International Latino Books Awards in the category of historical novels. It is taught in several universities. An adaptation of the novel into a play, produced under the direction of Virginia Aponte by Ago Teatro in Caracas in the spring and summer of 2014, and in Miami in the fall of the same year, was acclaimed by audiences and critics alike. It has since been staged in Madrid, Spain, in 2022 and 2023. Some of her short stories and a play have also been translated and appear in textbooks and anthologies such as *The Voice of the Turtle, Cuba: A Traveler's Literary Companion,*

Cubana: Contemporary Fiction by Cuban Women, and *Cuban American Theater.* For several years she contributed a weekly a column to *Diario Las Américas* and later to *El Nuevo Herald.* Her blog *Habanera soy* http://uvadearagon.wordpress.com is widely read. De Aragón has received several literary awards in the United States, Europe, and her native Cuba. Until her retirement in 2011, she was Associate Director of the Cuban Research Institute at Florida International University, where she also taught. Dr. de Aragón served for six years as Associate Editor of *Cuban Studies,* the most important academic journal focusing on Cuba. She obtained a Ph.D. in Latin American and Spanish Literature from the University of Miami. She is a corresponding member of the Academia Norteamericana de la Lengua Española (ANLE). Uva has lived in the United States since 1959. In 1999, she returned to Cuba for her first visit, and in subsequent years she has visited the island frequently, where her work has also been included in anthologies and literary magazines. She comes from a family of writers, has two daughters, four grandsons, and one great grandson.

Translators' Bios

Jeffrey C. Barnett is the S. Blount Mason Professor of Romance Languages at Washington and Lee University. Since 1989 he has taught classes on language, culture, and literature both domestically and abroad, including courses on the Spanish-American novel of the Boom, Caribbean literature, and literary translation. His articles on Spanish-American narrative and comparative literary studies have appeared in journals in Spain, Latin America, and the U.S. He has translated a diverse selection of Latin American authors, ranging from the short stories of Carlos Fuentes to the epic poetry of Martín del Barco Centenera. In addition to *The Memory of Silence*, his major book-length translations include *Rebaños* (2017)—a volume of poetry by Cuban author Zurelys López Amaya—as well as two other novels by de Aragón: *The Miracle of St. Lazarus* (2019) and, currently, *Murder on Biltmore Way*. He has lived in Honduras, Mexico, and Spain. When not in the classroom or translating, he spends his time on hiking trails pondering the nature of words.

Kathleen Bulger-Barnett is Professor of Modern Languages at the Virginia Military Institute, where she teaches both Spanish and Spanish American literature in addition to language and culture. She earned her Ph.D. from the University of Kentucky with a specialty in Spanish Golden Age drama and she teaches courses on Lope de Vega, Calderón de la Barca, and also Cervantes. She has a keen interest in Cuban literature and has presented research at various Caribbean conferences and has translated, together with Jeffrey C. Barnett, Uva de Aragon's *The Miracle of St. Lazarus,* and *Murder on Biltmore Way.* She is currently translating Uva de Aragon's *El reino de mi infancia.* In her free time, she gardens, hikes, travels, and recently completed her first two *caminos* on the Camino de Santiago, and looks forward to many more.

Index

www.ingramcontent.com/pod-product-compliance
Lightning Source LLC
Chambersburg PA
CBHW031939240626
47153CB00003B/788